From Beer to Paternity!

One man's journey through life as we know it.

GERRY BURKE

FROM BEER TO PATERNITY!
ONE MAN'S JOURNEY THROUGH LIFE AS WE KNOW IT.

iUniverse books may be ordered through booksellers or by contacting:

iUniverse
1663 Liberty Drive
Bloomington, IN 47403
www.iuniverse.com
844-349-9409

ISBN: 978-1-4401-3756-3 (sc)
ISBN: 978-1-4401-3757-0 (e)

Print information available on the last page.

iUniverse rev. date: 12/11/2020

ACKNOWLEDGEMENTS

Editing services Kylie Moreland

Charlie Chaplin image © Roy Export S.A.S.

Casbah illustration Erin Ruiz – Boise, Idaho

Lou Surfa illustration Frank Trobbiani – Melbourne, Australia

FOREWORD

Jerry Seinfeld used to position his television series as a show about nothing. It is now time for another Gerry to write a book about everything?

The author is a former advertising copywriter and Creative Director, who has practiced his craft in Britain, Australia, Asia and the U.S. His particular slant on the life that we all lead is a first person diatribe of opinions, nostalgia and fantasy-fuelled memories. Mr Burke has an impressive record of humor orientated achievements within the advertising industry, but until now, he has resisted the urge to release his archival collection of private invective for commercial consumption. "All for the general good" he says.

Unfortunately, with the financial crisis upon us, Gerry has reduced funds to maintain his current lifestyle. While I don't approve of this lifestyle, I can understand that race-horses, gambling, alcohol and the pursuit of wanton women can be a drain on one's finances. I don't, for one moment, believe his outrageous claims that he also needs to defend three Paternity Suits.

More than anybody, I subscribe to the theory that laughter is just the antidote for times like these and I know that Gerry would be disappointed if the following stories didn't tickle your funny bone, if not some other part of your anatomy.

Bill Shannon
Chairman
Melbourne International Comedy Festival

INTRODUCTION

When you are a single man, there are many opportunities to frequent bars, hotels and other licensed premises. It is a forum that allows one to formulate ideas and establish considered judgments. With each glass of beer, one acquires more confidence and it isn't long before you become an authority on the opposite sex, your fellow man and the community that exists for your sole gratification.

To avoid retribution, Gerry Burke often publishes under his pseudonym PEST. He provides commentary and opinion on Politics, Entertainment, Sport and Travel. Some of the following articles have been previously published. Others have not.

TABLE OF CONTENTS

RELATIONSHIPS!

Amour or Less!

From Beer to Paternity!

Sex Appeal!

I t was the end of the second week in February. My local pub was buzzing with activity and there were more couples in attendance than one usually expects. I was alone. All of the regulars had begged-off our ritual drinking session, due to commitments with wives and girlfriends. The pretty ladies, with their bonnets and baskets of roses, were acceptable eye-candy, but if they approached me one more time I would be forced to utter an expletive.

I had just been to a re-run of a great American war movie and was ready to expound my views to anyone who would listen. Oh well! It may as well be you.

AMOUR OR LESS!

We all have our favorite philosophers. For me, you just couldn't beat John Denver, who maintained that there are only two things that money can't buy – true love and home-grown tomatoes. Of course, JD was a bit of a softie. I've been hardened by a gruff and cantankerous demeanor, disgraceful manners and a voice that would frighten the most resolute maiden. Needless to say, I am not at my best on St Valentine's Day. After all, the very premise reeks of commitment, doesn't it? How they roped in poor old St Val, I'll never know. I'm betting that they cornered him in a rose arbor somewhere. Not that I've got anything against roses. I grow them myself.

I'm not such a beast as to openly ignore the occasion. All the same, if they want roses, they can help themselves. It's a self-service world. I know that many of my lady friends have been disappointed by my stance and have often intimated that this unromantic approach might get me a one-way ticket to a single bed. As confronting as this threatening ultimatum is, it was my teenage buddies who wounded me the most. They determined that I should go forward in life with the moniker *Pig*.

You are all probably wondering how one can put this into a romantic context. You can't. At the time, I always felt that you had to do what was expected of you. If I could instill a bit of swine fever into those almost accommodating virgins from the local Catholic sodality, it was the way to go. But who would fancy a guy in a paisley shirt and flares?

In places like Serbia and Croatia, they try to encourage romantic liaisons. Before you lift you first glass of wine, there will be a violin in your ear and the musician will only retire when money changes hands. In the Philippines, you get to meet the parents immediately after the first kiss. When things progress a bit further, aunts and uncles appear from nowhere. You then discover that they all coming on the honeymoon with you. One may have a bit of a giggle over the latter but the truth of the matter is that this commercial exploitation of female sensitivities could have serious consequences. What happens if February 14 falls on the same day as the *Dearly Precious Stakes* at Aqueduct?

OK! You're not the first person to tell me that I have my priorities all askew. Go ahead. Buy the rose. Make the commitment. Shall I put you down for five screaming kids, a mortgage you can't handle, the mother-in-law from hell and pot roast on Sundays? I still think that the Colorado cowboy had the right idea. Tomato soup ain't so bad.

FROM BEER TO PATERNITY!

B urt Lancaster was in uniform. Well, he was until he started cavorting with Deborah Kerr in the surf, on that hideaway beach near Pearl Harbor. I have never served in the forces but I reckon I would have needed a heart-starter to muster enough courage to mess with a senior officer's wife. I believe that he came straight from the Sergeant's Mess to their place of assignation.

From Here to Eternity was a best-selling book and the film won a bunch of awards, including one for Frank Sinatra. It was the first time that Hollywood had given us a true glimpse of the U.S. military, warts and all. Today, when major conflicts arise, the militia quarantine themselves. If you want any media information, a journalist is officially embedded into their midst.

The Second World War!

T here were American troops stationed in England, Australia and Japan and they all felt very isolated. Somebody came up with the idea that they should embed some girls into their midst. I believe it was the girls who came up with the idea. If you went for a beer with a G.I., you would end up with a good time and a pair of nylons. Nine months later, some gals ended up with a permanent memento of the occasion, but Daddy had probably moved on to Iwo Jima or some similar outpost. The classic account of this skirmish was appropriately called *Flags of our Fathers*. I know that I am going to cop some flak (sorry, Sergeant) by being so flippant about such a turbulent time in our lives. It wasn't all beer and skittles. It was beer and sex.

I sometimes question my own existence. I had blue eyes, a crew-cut and my old man was nowhere to be seen. Eventually, we found him down at the pub with his mates and it turned out that he wasn't a marine. Whereas the aforementioned novels were maritime ones, there were others that were not. Fraternization was still rife. Even with the enemy! I know a few very doubtful people who drink nothing but sake and if those Marx Brothers weren't commies, I don't know who was.

International policemen! That's what they are the yanks! If there's tension in Timbuktu, they'll be there. The Pres will make a commitment. MGM will make a movie and the soldiers will make some babies. It happened in East Germany, when the wall came down. Our media liaison officer was called Mr Schlitz and my stringer was Bud Weiser. Go on. Tell me that they weren't conceived in a velvet fog.

Some people will think that I'm digging up more filth than a waste management consultant but I am very wary of those people in the armed forces. Especially those submariners! What they get up to, down below, is nobody's business. Yes, I do have a solution. I think that soldiers and sailors should all drink sherry. I don't mean those big flagons. It is very difficult to consume one of those in a single sitting. Sherry is such a civilized drink. You can sip it and discuss art, instead of football and the barmaid with the big bazookas. Unless her name is also Sherry!

SEX APPEAL!

Right now, I am involved in one of those personal introspectives. I find that honest self-evaluation can sometimes help in situations like this. You see, I have just realized that I am completely ineffectual in my dealings with members of the opposite sex. It is true that I don't understand women but this is of little consequence. Hardly anybody that I know understands women. It is also true that I dither and drag the chain, a bit, when I try and engage the fair sex in meaningful conversation. They always seem to have the ability to rebuff my advances in a most finite manner and their economy of speech is most impressive. Sometimes, they only use two words.

I don't like to be too hard on myself because I am quite an urbane kind of guy, mildly sophisticated, artistically aware and recklessly wicked, if the need arises. So, what am I doing wrong? How do you get that female heart ticking?

He is suave, fearless and drives a sports car, but for the life of me, I can't see what ninety-nine sees in Maxwell Smart. He has no brains, no brawn and he isn't even rich. And herein lays the rub. Traditionally, if you have bad breath, stutter and wear highly magnified bifocals, you are up against it when trying to promote your personal magnetism. However, little Miss Hard-to-Please will waive these deficiencies if your name has recently appeared on the current rich list. She will not insist on a charisma bypass if you also happen to own a shoe factory. This is what we lamenting Lotharios are up against. All is not fair in love and war.

I am currently smitten with the perky young waitress at my local café. I suspect that she may have rings in her nipples and this excites me tremendously. There has been no dialogue, so far, as I fear that I may be vulnerable when attempting to converse in the modern idiom. I am comfortable with cool, sick and rack-off dirt-bag but if there have been advances in the essential vernacular, I will be lost. I also feel totally disadvantaged because I don't text.

If you have become a member of your country's Olympic team or played bass guitar for a rock band, you will not suffer the torment and self-doubt that I have gone though. And others like me! Many of us have toyed with the idea of becoming a celebrity, if that's what women want, but it is hard to raise your profile when you are getting on a bit. In fact, it is difficult to raise anything if you are past it. The alternative is to live with your memories and it may be necessary to color them with spin and exaggeration, if you really want a rush. Sex appeal quickly fades and what was once irresistible is now passé. Paul Newman's blue eyes were no longer required for the millennium time capsule and Johnny Depp's moustache is the new black.

Words fail me. Of course, that's where we started, isn't it? Given that I have a birthright that gives me legitimate access to a northern hemisphere colloquial communication called *Blarney*, my forebears will be grossly disappointed that I did not carry the baton, as they would have expected. A man without a woman is sad. The reverse is even worse. According to renowned feminist Gloria Steinem "a woman without a man is like a fish without a bicycle."

– II –

RESPECT AND DEVOTION!

Oh my God!

Little Women!

We all have to be very careful when we wax lyrical in the public arena. I hope that none of my opinions are interpreted as being sexist, as I certainly regard myself as being gender tolerant. Nevertheless, one has to tread lightly. As with religion!

The Catholic Hour was a tradition in the place where I was brought up. We convened after Holy Mass on Sunday and the Vice-President of the football club always tapped the keg. Unfortunately, the President was always late, as he was committed to hearing confessions after mass. You may wonder, with such a pedigree, that one would find the need to question one's faith. Nevertheless, it happens.

OH MY GOD!

They say that truth is stranger than fiction; you only have to look at one's life journey to confirm this. The road we travel is hard and long and perpetually punctuated by the potholes of personal tragedy. Just when you are starting to get comfortable with someone, they are taken from you in inexplicable circumstances. I highlight the disappearance of Glenn Miller, Amelia Earhart, Lord Lucan and Michael Jackson. You need faith to get through it all and heaven can help.

We all have defining moments in our life. During my last trip to Dublin, I was in O'Connell St. and feeling a bit hungry. I spied a middle-aged street vendor promoting his produce in front of his fruit stall. He was an Orangeman but not from Ulster. I purchased a dozen juicy ones. When I sat down in the park to give myself an infusion of vitamin C, I noticed that there were only eleven oranges in the bag. This really got my Irish up and I stormed back to the lily-livered weasel who had sold me the fruit. He had found a bad orange and thrown it out for me.

From that day forth, I became a very suspicious person. An avid theatergoer, I now steer away from productions like *Twelfth Night*, *12 Angry Men* and *Cheaper by the Dozen*. I am even re-evaluating my religion. JC seems all right but what about those twelve apostles? There is a bad egg in there, somewhere. I am presently thinking Scientology but my current partner is a devout Roman Catholic and she is not interested in meeting Tom Cruise or John Travolta. Not until hell freezes over she vehemently wails.

Hell! Now there is a concept that I find very off-putting and being a marketing sage, I am amused that the Vatican would want to use it as a unique selling proposition to increase their flock. Who wants to commit on the back of fear and trepidation? Being a horse racing man, I would feel more comfortable with Allah, who, I am told, has a fine stable of Arabians and many camels. I think that some of them may have been indentured to me in a former life.

I won't even attempt to flirt with the Hindu religion or Buddhism. It's those orange robes. I carry emotional scars. Needless to say, they also ask a lot of you. Nirvana sounds like a pretty cool place but their insistence on zero tolerance in relation to sensual enjoyment goes beyond the pale. If you can't get your rocks off, how do you find inner peace? Do they want you to become a monk or something? On the credit side, I do like the chanting. If Hare Krishna could get a cheer squad together, it would be just right for the Colorado Crush.

Some of you may think that I am a bit paranoid. Just because I have been shortchanged by a callous and avaricious merchant, I am prepared to forsake the only one who loves me (there was a dog, once). In truth, I have been crushed by this Dublin experience. My absolute belief in fair play and the nobility of merchandising has been shattered. This is the worst kind of wealth creation: greed. Given his head, I can see that entrepreneurial Irish weasel moving on to the Big Apple or even out west. In Orange County, the produce never goes bad and I am sure that he would have a good time at Anaheim with like-minded souls. I have been to Disneyland and there are disreputable Leprechauns everywhere.

This esoteric excursion that I have taken you on may not deepen your own religious convictions and I can understand that. The road I travel is fraught with contradictions and I am probably not the right person to advise you if you have doubts about your own journey. Let's face it. When Moses came down from the mountain with those two tablets, they were bitter pills to swallow. What! You can't covet your neighbor's house! Or his wife! There was no mention of the cutey that lives in the next street. She's a peach.

LITTLE WOMEN!

Haven't read the original? Don't bother. I can bring you up to date, with all that needs to be said. As a young man, I was not an academic heavyweight. All the same, my parents held high hopes that I would become a brain surgeon or a rocket scientist. When these lofty career targets did not eventuate, there was no apparent disappointment. They still thought that I was brilliant. Before you protest, let me say that I don't think that this is the time or the place for alternative opinions, from non-family sources. Let us just say that one doesn't need to be smart to be a smarty-pants. However, you do need to be bright to be brilliant.

Recently, some Arab gentleman paid Kylie Minogue four million dollars to headline the opening of his new hotel in Dubai. I firmly believe that I could have raised that kind of money to stop her from singing. Now, don't get me wrong. I love the gal. She is five feet nothing in her stockings and always punching above her weight.

What is it about diminutive women? History is rich with definitive literary interpretations of female superiority amongst the height deficient. Before Louisa May Alcott came along, there was Little Red Riding Hood, Joan of Arc and Hannah the Barbarian. Was this the start of feminism or just the feisty attitude that we now know and love so much?

When you are a small boy, everyone seems big. I know that I was devastated to discover that all the other cowboys had to stand in a hole to make Alan Ladd look tall. In later years, I laughed when somebody suggested that Pamela Anderson and Dolly Parton weren't that big. Nevertheless, they were centimeter perfect. It is always hard to define the perfect package and I would hesitate to elicit an assessment on this subject from any of my female friends. The response would be understandably frosty. Why do my young friends think that I am deliriously happy when I tell them that I have a real cool relationship?

There are some of us who don't project all that well and this may be down to an inferiority complex, abject stuttering or just plain baldness. In situations like this, you always need a good woman behind you. Someone with more balls than a female juggler! If Jesse James had little Annie Oakley behind him instead of that cad who shot him in the back, he may still be alive today. All of five feet, Annie was a legend in her own lifetime. With a pistol, rifle or shotgun she could hit a dime at ninety feet. She was even more accurate when aiming at cheating husbands.

Elizabeth Taylor just divorced them. There were eight marriages in all and she was usually the one who had to pay alimony. On the other hand, Zsa Zsa Gabor (nine marriages) was always on the money. That is why many people assumed that she was from the Check Republic. In fact, the lady was Hungarian and although marginally more statuesque than Liz, they were on a level playing field with their quotable quotes. "Conrad Hilton was very generous to me in the divorce settlement. He gave me five thousand Gideon Bibles." Ms Taylor's first husband was Mr Hilton's son, so Zsa Zsa was her mother-in-law.

Let's hear it for the mother-in-law. Is there a crescendo of applause for the most unappreciated and misunderstood creatures on the planet? Sadly not! The seeds of distrust have been long planted. "He that would the daughter win must with the mother first begin." I don't know who wrote this little gem, but it smacks of prose that grows from frustration and disappointment. Obviously the prospective suitor didn't have a weak heart and a chain of hotels. This would just about tick all the boxes.

I hate to end this absorbing dissertation on such a confrontational note but the truth of the matter is that we fellas don't understand women much at all. I should know more by the time I have completed research on my next project. It is called *Big Girls*.

– III –

TELEVISION!

The Idiot Box!

Desire and Envy!

Most of the rooms in my house boast a television sct. Except the toilet! Some would say that I acquired the wrong feng shui expert. Nevertheless, one can never ignore one of the great communication tools of out time. Those of you who possess a less imposing number of units are likely to experience family disturbances of immense proportions. It is rare that your teenage daughter will share viewing preferences with any of her siblings, her mother or the dog or cat.

Nobody wants to watch any of the stuff that you hold sacred. That is why you always appreciate the heaven-sent opportunity to retire to the pub, where the sports channel is on permanent hold.

THE IDIOT BOX!

I recently spent a whole day in bed, watching television. No, I wasn't doing research for my forthcoming article on sloth. Yours truly was feeling poorly and also a little irritable. My rude awakening was courtesy of a hungry animal on the end of my bed who confirmed his presence in the usual manner: a bite on the toe followed by a face-lick!

What I really don't like about morning television is the fact that everyone is so bloody happy. The terrible twins have been out of bed since sparrow-fart and if they can't have a good lie-in, neither will you. And all that bonhomie with the newsreader! Give us a break. The whole presentation team could appear naked and I wouldn't even notice. I am totally mesmerized by the clock. It ticks away in perpetuity, an engrossing watermark of unspoken guilt and insinuation. "Come on, you slob. Get out of bed. There's work to be done."

I couldn't start my day until I was secure in the knowledge that Brad and Angelina had resolved their differences with Jen. The extroverted Hollywood reporter would leave no stone unturned to provide this kind of information, but I do suspect that they wait two weeks and then replay the same gossip again. The intervening hours until the midday movie started were excruciating. I couldn't help but think that housework must be a real turn-off if people had to resort to these kinds of entertainment options.

Movies at midday are mostly mundane. They are mainly derived from dross and spillage of B-grade releases, box-office failures, made-for-television rubbish and mindless budget vehicles for desperate thespians. It can be tedious torment and the challenge for the viewer is to make it to the first ad break. Nevertheless, this time, I was up for it.

There have been many crass aviation films but this was worse than most. The flick was made in Australia with unknown American actors. I loved it when the villain made a dash for freedom from his Bondi hotel directly onto the concourse of the Sydney Opera House. Only the locals would know that this is geographically impossible. It was a shame that they couldn't include a shot of Ayers Rock in the scene, but the harbor bridge was in the background and I thought I saw a kangaroo jump out of the water. Then again, it may just have been a bit of subliminal advertising from their airline sponsor.

If I could be slightly critical of the presentation, I would have to say that the ads were far too long. By the time we got back to the plane, the captain only had three seconds to disarm the bomb. He did it but for the life of me I couldn't understand why he didn't just ask the passengers for help. We have seen so many of these potboilers, we all know exactly what to do. Just don't cut the red wire. In essence, I applaud creative license and have even dabbled myself. I wrote this terrific screenplay about the Pope winning a gold medal at the Senior Olympics. Unfortunately, the Catholic Church is demanding creative control, so that one is going nowhere.

Enough about me! What about the medium? It is certainly not rare, but daytime television is acceptable if you are elderly, frail, work nights or the temperature is less than temperate. Let's be brutally frank here. You know that the roses need pruning. The front gate has a loose hinge and what about all those leaves that need sweeping? On top of that, it is almost ninety degrees and the nymphomaniac next door is sun-baking topless by the pool.

Time moved on and my friends, who are well aware of my distain for the early evening productions which masquerade as news commentary, dropped-off the chicken broth. They didn't stick around for the tirade that was sure to come. Some years ago, I discovered my old gran watching one of these horrible current affair programs. "What are you doing?" I cried. "You are an intelligent woman. Why watch this crap?" When she didn't reply, I felt a deep surge of contrition. Perhaps she had just nodded off during the news. In point of fact, she had been dead for three days and this is the kind of thing that can happen to you when you are indiscriminate with your entertainment choices.

The format is always the same. Some greasy slime-bag has defrauded an incapacitated widow out of her life savings and the news hound from the OB van is out for the kill. Not only does he ram a microphone up the culprit's nose, but continues to harass the poor scoundrel through his front door, down the hall, out past the kitchen and into what is usually the sanctity of his outdoor thunderbox. If the budget allows, they will divert the traffic chopper into the vicinity in order to get a different perspective on the situation. By this time, I am well and truly rooting for the besieged. For some reason, this little charade will mesmerize viewers across the nation and the next morning, a crude, boorish cigar-chomping TV executive will be salivating over the official ratings of the aforementioned interlude. Above his head, a framed quotation provides the raison d'être for his incredible success as an analyst of market share and audience gratification – *Never overestimate the intelligence of the viewer.*

Bring on prime time or take me now, I implored the good Lord, knowing full well that our savior was relaxed and even a bit smug with the ratings figures for *Songs of Praise*: an ecclesiastical favorite!

I have never much cared for dead bodies. Now I have to flush them out of my television monitor every week and medical examiners have become the matinee idols of the morgue. Obviously, we have rather macabre viewing habits, but shouldn't there be some disclaimer about not trying this at home? Children are very inquisitive and it may be that scalpels are now outselling HB pencils. I have even been involved in such procedures myself. A few weeks ago, I accidentally dropped a slab of tinnies on my cat. He must have died of shock because it was definitely light beer. This was a wonderful opportunity to conduct a post mortem, but I have to say, it was less than fulfilling. Even so, I did discover what happened to Johnny next door's pet hamster.

Some people seem to think that life after death makes for riveting entertainment and so we have any number of programs about the supernatural, aliens and vampire slayers. I have to tell you, folks. This is all fantasy. Get a life. If only they could breathe some new life into those traditional formats. One of those crime franchises must have been running for over forty years. In fact, the desk sergeant at my local precinct told me that there have been more actors in the homicide division than law enforcement officers.

Am I being less than kind? Television is a mind-numbing diversion that rarely provides quality entertainment, even in the ratings period. The masters of the game continually insult their audiences with program over-runs and sleight-of-hand programming. I don't have to tell you how they let the cat out of the bag with their reality television. Until the introduction of this phenomenon, we had no idea that there were so many dead-beats and ding-bats in this country.

Prime time usually finishes with a whimper, rather than a bang. If you have been dating seriously, this is where you discover whether your future partner has somnolent problems.

I often drift off due to boredom and was under the misapprehension that I could get away with it. My squeeze called in CSI Brighton Beach and I subsequently learned that my level of snoring was a real glass-breaker.

Nevertheless, some people are never bored and really get off on it. The other evening, I was squeezed into my peak-hour transit convenience and the young lass seated beside me was on her cell phone; rabbiting-on about the saga that was the previous night's edition of *Big Brother*. Even the heavily pregnant lady who was hanging from a strap in front of me was captivated. I spied a copy of the *TV Guide* protruding from one of her many parcels. I'll bet that she couldn't wait to get home and kick off her shoes and who could blame her? Standing all the way, on the subway, in her condition, must have been tough.

I don't expect that my career as a television reviewer will be a long one. I always maintain that one should be completely honest but this is not always appreciated by those who have vested interests. There are even those people who have opinions that differ from mine. I am currently trying to get my head around this kind of thinking.

DESIRE AND ENVY!

One of my dear friends always claimed that she was born to show business and was disappointed that she had never become a household name. Given that her surname was Hoover, I felt that she was short-changing herself. Especially as that other household name, Simpson, made it big time, with residuals.

I was hoping that this delightful lady might have done better because throughout my own illustrious life I have never been able to establish a relationship with anyone who might be colloquially called a television personality. However, I did live in hope and sequentially lusted over Darlene and Annette from the *Mickey Mouse Club*, all the barrel girls, including Princess Panda and a host of vocalists, teenage adventure presenters and finally, the girls from the Playboy Mansion.

I think Letterman, O'Brien and Jay Leno may have called a few times, but I wasn't interested. Nevertheless, I was fascinated by the appeal and familiarity that was established between the showman and the viewer. Really! Did we have anything in common with these people? I didn't think so. They were and still are extroverts. When someone introduced reality television we discovered that we could be entertained by watching somebody do something that was completely boring and innocuous. If there were similarities to your own tedious escapades, you could wallow in your own mediocrity.

I was brought up to appreciate performance skills and that is why I was always in the front row whenever the circus came to town. They would pitch their tent, assemble their Ferris wheel and put on the show of a lifetime. With no fanfare at all, they would then dismantle everything and move to another town. Can you believe that England's giant Ferris wheel, the London Eye, cost over one hundred million dollars? Go on. Poke me in the eye with a pencil. How could it cost one hundred million dollars?

Television is a cheap night in. Everybody loves Raymond, Frasier and the Boogaloo Sisters, which are best appreciated with take-out pizza or homemade pastrami on rye. In Australia, you can serve up bubble and squeak to kith and kin and watch *Kath and Kim*, with no thought of recrimination. One man's meat is another man's poison. However, the thought that the aforementioned are all entertainment millionaires fills me with envy and disappointment in my own less-than-brilliant career. It all looked so good when I was playing the spoons for grandpa at the O'Reilly Christmas party. He was so complimentary and, after all, he did an occasional solo with *McNamara's Band*, didn't he?

I saw my first television broadcast through a shop window and was oblivious to the fact that the whole industry was flying by the seat of their pants. It wasn't all that obvious to us because we were in awe of this fabulous technological miracle from America. It was only a matter of time before our local heroes made it onto the silver screen. Unfortunately, they never did but Roy Rogers and the Lone Ranger were more than acceptable replacements. My mother often remarked that I bore an uncanny resemblance to Roy, but she thought that he had a better singing voice. This grated on me a bit – particularly, during one episode when he started playing the spoons!

In those days, you could probably get on television if you had a bit of chutzpah. Today, you have to stand in line and do your thing. *American Idol*, *Dancing Dingoes* and *Make me a Supermodel* are all indicative of the fact that the circus is back in town. Some of them are pretty good but their appeal no longer resonates. Sure, my era went crazy for the Beatles and even ABBA, but the goal posts have changed. Everything is so motivated by marketing and one only feels sympathy for the guileless and gormless, who have been garroted by promises of gratification and glory.

I think the glory days of television are over. The sets are bigger and clearer but the content remains murky. As Sam Goldwyn used to say "a wide screen makes a bad film twice as bad." I fear for my declining years. If Ted Turner's classic movies are no longer around, I may have to rely on my young nurse to provide entertainment alternatives, on a cold winter night. The summer will be OK. I still have my surfboard.

Harriet Hoover

– IV –

ANIMALS!

One evening last week!

My favorite girl!

"K9 to Control"

My relationship with domestic pets has been erratic. I have loved them. Now, I loathe them. Whoa! Wait a minute. This is an extreme statement. Let us just say that I cannot fit them into my busy schedule. My preference is for the four-legged beast which has income-producing potential and possible residual value. Yes, I am obsessed with horse racing. The extent of my participation will be apparent as you read on. Unfortunately, my creditors have been able to run faster than most of the animals I have owned. However, there have been exceptions.

I have lived in quite a number of places. My family eventually established permanent roots but I had already contracted the bug called wanderlust. It was always difficult to overcome my fear of flying but when I did, I delighted in the joys associated with living in another country. Today, you may still run into me at the White Rooster Bar in Los Angeles or the convivial Slug and Lettuce in London. Who said I don't like animals?

ONE EVENING LAST WEEK!

The other evening, I was beachside, taking in one of those wonderful sunsets which are commonplace in our particular suburban paradise. On the golden sands was a frolicking ratepayer, who only had eyes for his faithful companion and the far horizon. Every time he hurled this stick out into the water, the confused canine dog-paddled out and retrieved it.

I recognized the humanoid as a neighbor of mine and had to question why a man with such impressive medical qualifications would derive such pleasure from this simplistic ritual? There is a general chain of thought that the animals may be smarter than we think. Perhaps they only engage in this type of repetitive activity because they think that we're stupid and they are prepared to humor us. Consider this. They pay no board, get free meals and accommodation and are pampered with indulgent grooming and constant petting. Who's the dummy then?

You have probably deduced that I am not a person who needs the company of a panting pal or a salivating chum to help me make it through the day. I used to be such a person but no more. I realize that they are a wonderful diversion for the little people and dogs with aggressive natures are indispensable as a deterrent to those who would contemplate a life of crime. I have heard that Inspector Rex is up for promotion and well deserved, too. But it's not just the dribbling that I don't like. There used to be a Detective Slobberwitz in one of those New York television shows and he was alright. All the same, he didn't have a cold nose. How can you love someone with a cold nose?

One of my associates had this huge dog called Hamlet. I don't know what breed he was but he was the great bane of her life and an irritation to her many friends. One day he chewed right through her priceless Dhurry. Yes, you guessed it. The one with the fringe on top! For some inexplicable reason, he received complete and total forgiveness. A few months earlier, I threw up on the damn thing and she tossed me out.

Although I am sometimes a little envious of the special relationship that our dish licking friends have with members of the opposite sex, I am in no way bitter – just a little animal intolerant! I definitely have issues with some of their habits relating to bodily functions. In sporting circles, the pundits are happy to proclaim "whatever happens on the field stays on the field" and I applaud one of their few poetic masterpieces. In the dog world, *Best in Show* often leaves a legacy on their field of endeavor that is hard to ignore. It is also hard to get it off your shoes when you get home.

Many of my readers will have fond memories of those canine superstars that made it to Hollywood and carved their name in glory. I refer to Lassie, Rin Tin Tin and at least 101 Dalmatians. Their time at the top was a tribute to their excellent work ethic and their unpretentious attitude to fame and fortune. Whilst other graduates of the studio star system were difficult and demanding, these pampered pooches required nothing more than a bit of filet mignon and a water bowl.

The only reason that I defer to Hollywood in this thought provoking article is that this is where I turn to try and get an angle on relationships. There may be more pertinent opinions around but they never seem to appear in the gossip mags. The relationship between man and mongrel is still a mystery to me and as long as it remains so, I will not be contemplating brain surgery with any stick-throwing surgeon from my neighborhood. However, some of my contemporaries have suggested that this might be a good idea.

MY FAVORITE GIRL!

I have to be quite honest. Beatrice is rather plain. Under no circumstances could you classify her as a beauty. Her head is too small. Her rear end is too big. There is something funny about one of her legs and she has an oral hygiene problem. On top of that, she is often embarrassing to be with. Flatulence can be so disconcerting. Nevertheless, I love her dearly.

Some of you will be cynical and put my devotion down to avaricious greed, rather than honest gratitude and unqualified admiration of her ability to bring home a winner's check. Obviously, Beatrice is her stable name. I would like to withhold her registered identity, in order to protect the innocent.

Innocent is such a confrontational word, isn't it? Over the years, we have heard it eloquently expressed from the mouths of Conrad Black, Lindsay Lohan and even Fatty Arbuckle. Down in her day yard, Beatrice was singularly uninterested in our country's jurisprudence system, although she was aware that a controversial Supreme Court judge enjoyed a ten percent ownership in her half brother, the hurdler. The gelding wasn't always a hurdler. He was the highest priced yearling of his year, but when he didn't win any races on the flat, he became a hurdler. When he didn't win any hurdle races, I was able to buy Beatrice for a song. Eventually, she was grateful but our first meeting at the track didn't go well. She broke two bones in my foot but I think that she was just trying to assert her independence. Once she learned that I was signing all the checks for her vitamin additives and chemical infusions we were at peace.

From my experience, women seem more interested in relationships than men, but I don't think female horses care one jot. If you've got a carrot in your hand, you're going to be the man most likely. That's how I schmoozed my way into her psyche and she reciprocated by bankrolling my champagne and chips lifestyle at the local casino. That big ass of hers continually catapulted her past any number of wannabes and into the pages of posterity. I became a constant in her life. Some of her trainers were not. When her penultimate mentor departed, to spend time at a correctional institution, the new man brought in a fresh team. He was not appreciative of some of the initiatives that had been introduced and immediately discontinued her vegetable diet. Beatrice's form has since tapered off and I have been left with many crates of performance enhancing carrots, which I had sourced from a Sicilian friend in New York.

Now she wants to start a family and it is going to be down to me to find her a mate for her forthcoming visit to the breeding barn. It's fair to say that these guys have no objections to making out on a first date and I hope that she is mentally prepared for this kind of equine gigolo.

I hate paying for sex and some of these hyped-up stallions carry a pretty hefty price tag. On the other hand, I've always been a soft touch. And she is my favorite girl.

"K9 TO CONTROL"

The entertainment options in your living room were probably similar to ours. Cops and robbers shows were the staple diet of the television programmer and we were sucked in to Colombo, Kojak, Morse and Miss Marple. I became convinced that I would end up as an unrelenting law enforcer with a bent for trouble. Or even a private-eye! As it turned out, my shadow never crossed the portals of any police recruitment agency. Nevertheless, I was privileged to lock horns with one of the most gifted detectives of all time. Inspector Rex was stationed at headquarters in Vienna when I experienced my initial confrontation with the local constabulary.

A speeding ticket!

The Homicide Squad turned out to be where the Traffic Infringement Office should have been and I was immediately set upon by the wonder dog. In no time at all, I was spread-eagled on the floor and staring at four 9 mm Heckler and Koch P30s. It was only after Kommisar Rex started licking my face that the tension decreased. That left-over bratwurst that I was saving for an afternoon snack was the magnet that had attracted Austria's finest. For all fifteen citations that he had been awarded, the felons had food on or about their person when arrested. In the end we became friends and every morning he used to bound over to my hotel with a rolled-up copy of the *Alsatian News* in his mouth. It was almost impossible to get French newspapers from Alsace in this city. I don't know how he did it.

Much has been said about the canine capacity to comprehend different languages and Rex was better than most. Prior to his transfer to the Justice Department, he was working border security for Customs and Immigration and had to match wits with unscrupulous offenders from many countries. Who can forget when he apprehended that Japanese diplomat who was trying to smuggle diamonds across the border, hidden in his lunch box? Unfortunately, the evidence was destroyed when Rex ate the sushi. He did, however, manage to pass the stones a few days later.

It's a dirty job but somebody has to do it. That is why my panting friend is where he is today. His employers get unconditional commitment and total devotion to duty. Rex makes things happen. He sticks his cold nose into places where others fear to go. He is brave, tireless, enthusiastic and uncompromising. Sadly, he tends to overact a bit. Nevertheless, there is an edge to his performances that cannot be ignored. Once Americans warm to this vigilante from Vienna, a trip to the Kodak Theater may not be so far off. At least, he must be one of the favorites for a *Golden Water Bowl* award and that's not to be sniffed at.

I suspect that there are many sides to this engaging crime fighter and I suppose a really good investigative journalist would have pushed the envelope a little further. What about the myth behind the mutt? Was there life outside the bureau? Or that rumored love interest! Were those sexy Rexy comments just office scuttlebutt?

I never got to find out. They cancelled my visa and had me deported. I should never have chosen to foxtrot during one of their beloved waltzes. If the inspector had been awake he could have interceded on my behalf but he was snoring in front of the log fire. It is always better to let sleeping dogs lie. I never saw him again.

– V –

HOME AND AWAY!

Table for one!

If I could walk on water!

When you live alone, as I do, there is rarely anyone around to listen to your opinions on anything. Sometimes it is good to get away and meet new people who can immediately fill the void. I believe that the best captive audiences can be found on boats and in jail cells. Alternatively, one can always write a book and that is what I have done. Unfortunately, you can sometimes get ahead of yourself. You really shouldn't be considering the film adaptation until you are convinced that you will sell more than a dozen copies of the paperback.

Right now, I am going to invite you into my home and you can observe the creative process, first hand. Perhaps my subject matter could have been more exciting but I usually just go with the flow. I often like to ruminate during my evening meal. It is a period when I am at peace with the world and the moments are free from incessant interruption. It is also a dangerous time of day. Sometimes the ambiance takes over and the lines become a little blurred. If you have more than two glasses of wine with dinner, they become very blurred.

TABLE FOR ONE!

In many societies, the first born male is endowed with a bequest of ultimate wealth and succession. His siblings inherit the wind. As a favorite son, I looked forward to such a reward and was enthused by my father's canny investment skills. He said he was putting all his money into Irish whiskey and I mistakenly assumed that he was talking about the stock market. In the end, I became heir to volumes of Gaelic literature, breakable dinnerware and some dubious looking photographs of his glory days in the IRA.

The years went by and the family tree became laden with priests, nuns, spinsters and grumpy old men. My star ascended. I was favored as the keeper of their treasured possessions and my humble abode became the repository for all their heirlooms and memorabilia. No cash, but lots of crockery! The silver service, bone china and elegant finery of the lace table cloths are redolent of a bygone era, where gentle folk cherished every moment that they would spend at the dinner table.

One evening, as I was picking at my banana fritter, I couldn't help but think what manner of wonderful sights and sounds my dinner set has witnessed over all these years. I have never underestimated inanimate objects and although they have not been gifted with speech facilities, one should never assume that their powers of observation are inadequate. To cut a long story short, I immediately realized the potential of a tome on the subject, with a screen treatment to follow. The prospective page-turner was entitled *My Life as a Plate*. It was quickly researched, written and submitted to a gullible publisher.

I had long harbored ambitions to write the quintessential novel about soup and I felt that this was the right course to take at this time. I reckoned that if I could get it out there, it would be all aboard for the gravy train and Hollywood, here we come. I wondered if Lillian Dish was still alive. She would be perfect for the female lead.

With most things entrepreneurial, timing is everything. The day before I went to pitch my new novel, Paris Hilton was there with hers: *My Life as a Fashion Plate*. What a bummer!

When I returned home with the devastating news, the inhabitants of my cutlery drawer were positively livid. Here was the cutting edge technology of the nineteenth century and they had a story to tell. The butter dishes and jam jars were similarly miffed. The economy was tight and they needed the bread. Now we were all hamstrung by a particularly pre-eminent, peripatetic personality, with limited life experience. Judging by the general mood, one could guess that she might also have limited life expectancy. Although I can honestly say that I did nothing to encourage it, the knives were out for Paris and I soon found a dinner invitation on my bureau, addressed to the lady in question. If she didn't bring along one of her supermodel pals, all Elle would break loose.

You can tell by the way this yarn is heading that any bird that enters these premises will be earmarked for Christmas or Thanksgiving. That's why I think it is imperative that I contact Wes Craven before they commit to a storyline for *Scream 7*. *The Attack of the Killer Tomatoes* was good but how could it compare with *The Jars that Ate Paris?*

Before this all got ugly, I had invited my lawyer over for a salt and battery hen and she liked that. It was a nice way to discuss the ramifications of my intellectual property in an intimate atmosphere. Unfortunately, the ears of corn, which I had served as an accompaniment, picked up on our conversation and relayed it to the tart with the nice pear, on the dessert tray. It wasn't long before the whole table was aware of my masterpiece and wanted some of the action. They were even geared up for the Hollywood production. Many of them had previous experience as props and eighty percent of them had a Green Card. I had never seen crockery and utensils so animated. They were carrying on like the pepperazzi at the opening of a salmon farm.

My book was never published. And where's Craven? Or Paris Hilton! They never came to dinner. History has many stories and the moral to this one is to never dine alone. Fantasy, Ireland and a banana fritter was an adagio of danger that had me dancing with the devil. Maybe I was destined to get caught up in the cobwebs of time? Perhaps my forbears could have begat more children but I think I know why they didn't. That antique egg timer in my kitchen hasn't worked since 1942. Neither have I.

IF I COULD WALK ON WATER!

When my father decided to immigrate to the country of my birth, I don't think anybody told him that the place was a bloody island. He probably didn't care. I know that he left his mother country in a hurry and my own mother sort of confirmed that. She said that he was breathing heavily when he arrived. Then again, so were her other suitors. She was a most attractive woman.

Water is so much part of our culture. We always have to consider it whenever we depart the country. You are either up, up and away or you're bob, bob, bobbin' along. I don't like planes much. Boats are fine until they get holes in them. Oh dear! Travel is such a gamble.

I dipped my toe into the brine at an early age and was able to swim to the wreck off-shore from our local beach. I was never really confident in my swimming prowess and I often think about that wreck. In fact, I thought about it, last week, when my travel agent booked me on a Mediterranean cruise!

I'm a bit of a pier fisherman and I thought that it would be nice to see Sardinia or Tunisia. Maybe go all the way to Salmonella. Nevertheless, I think that she detected that there was a little nervousness there. Booking the connecting flight was bad enough as I also have a fear of flying and there are a number of issues that concern me. Mainly, things relating to gravity, aircraft maintenance and pilots on work experience! Last year, they had to disentangle me from the stewardess when we hit an air-pocket. She claimed that I didn't have enough frequent flyer points for the Mile High Club.

My salacious days are gone. I am now half-way between senility and serendipity, which is a fate worse than death. Thus, the senior's sailathon! I can picture the new me lazing away on deck with a good book, Morocco bound. I wonder if *Rick's Café Américaine* is still the place to be seen in Casablanca. Some people may think that I live in the past but it has taken me this long to attempt another water crossing. The good Lord chose not to make me a fearless person or give me wings. Our Supreme Being could walk on water. I saw football legend Ron Barassi walk on water. Why can't I walk on water?

It is best to focus on the positive side of sea travel and people tell me that the food is always excellent. They stop short of endorsing the vittles in North Africa but I have seen Alfred Hitchcock's version of *The Man Who Knew Too Much*. I'm pretty sure that he didn't die from food poisoning. This kind of travel is all about fine dining and I know that my heart is never far from my stomach. However, I will probably harbor suspicions if the offerings don't look absolutely kosher. How do you compare the egg roll that you had on the boardwalk at Atlantic City with the Plat du Jour on the Marrakesh Express? You can't. One is wholesome home-cooked chow. The other is just fast food.

My friends tell me that vehicles are highly unreliable in these conditions and that the camel is the best means of travel. If you stick to camels, you'll be really smokin' but leave it there. Don't let anyone introduce you to Mr Hashish. Perhaps, I'll just stay on the ship. Oh Lord! Wings would be helpful or even the Mary Poppins travel option. That umbrella of hers didn't need any gas or a road for that matter. It had silent running and protection against the elements. Unfortunately, people could see up her dress. That must have been embarrassing.

– VI –

THE SILVER SCREEN!

A Hitch in Time!

Funny Business!

Cowboys!

As a youngster, I spent a lot of time at the movies. Who didn't? If you wanted to suck face with your best friend's little sister, this is where the opportunity would arise. In earlier times, our whole gang headed for the front stalls and we didn't miss a thing.

So, here we are. A thousand years later and it is tribute time. My young readers will be perplexed and wonder what this is all about but how can you describe nostalgia? I like to think that it is a wistful melancholy that can only be exacerbated by thoughtful reminiscing. The following articles can be taken with food and drink. Popcorn and soda pop are recommended.

A HITCH IN TIME!

Hitchcock was his name and he was the master of suspense. His heroes were the matinee idols of their day. And his leading ladies? Well, they were mostly blonde, weren't they? And expendable! Janet was stabbed, poor Grace was nearly strangled and the lovely Tippi was almost pecked to death by those damn birds.

I was a young, impressionable youth when *Psycho* first hit our screens and Janet Leigh was a Hollywood star of great magnitude. In those days, it was unthinkable to carve up a good looking babe so early in a picture. Not only that but she was naked. I realize that this is an acceptable code of undress for people who are bathing but we were not used to seeing nudity on screen. I think that shower scene was the precursor to what we now know as soap opera. He was a real trailblazer.

Few directors were as prolific as Hitch. His career spanned five generations and although we now look back at the technology and cringe, he always directed with great panache. They say that you should never work with children or animals and yet, the way he directed all those birds was a tribute to patience and his desire for perfection. The two minute scene in which Tippi Hedren is attacked took a whole week to shoot. The shower scene with Janet probably only needed two minutes but I reckon he may have taken a week. This film left its mark on me. I still refuse to shower alone.

Alfred was also a prolific actor. He appeared in every film that he made, but only fleetingly. Often with children and animals! He had an hour-glass figure but it was obvious that most of his hours had been spent eating. He soon became a caricature of himself, which became the opening credits of his popular television show. A haunting musical score and his dramatic introduction gave fair warning that our blood pressure was about to rise. We dimmed the living room lights.

Music and sound effects are part of the mix with every well-made movie and Hitchcock used or didn't use them to great effect. If you suffer from vertigo, you wouldn't want to plunge to your death without a musical accompaniment would you? No, you wouldn't and the director knew that. He preferred sound effects because he said that he didn't have a musical ear and this is evident because he cast Doris Day in one of his movies. But, she was blonde and that appeared to be one of his casting priorities.

I think about murder a lot and I do have a short list. Some of them are even people I don't know. However, attempting something like this can be a life changing experience and you need to think the whole thing through. The introduction of DNA has made it more difficult to get away with the kind of dastardly deeds that preoccupied our predecessors but Hitch was the kind of guy who could always come up with something novel.

It is true that many of Alfred's leading players were quite notorious for their irrational behavior. Norman Bates was mentally fragile. Others were just emotionally compromised. Marnie actually swooned at the sight of blood. He was adept at maximizing suspense and that is why many of his screenplays were melodramatic rather than overt. In *Rear Window* there was hardly a scene change but we didn't even notice. On top of that, the film went twenty minutes longer than it should have because Jimmy Stewart stuttered. I saw this masterpiece with my friend Rebecca, who subsequently discovered binoculars in my bedroom and accused me of being a pervert and a snoop. Some years later, I met her at the races and she apologized.

I don't know much about the psychology of fear but the fat little man from England did. He liked to continually prove that everything is not what it seems. We all take away something different from a Hitchcock film. To me, there are two obvious lessons to be learnt from his entertaining legacy of celluloid magic. Blondes are more trouble than they are worth and a boy should always love his mother. Nevertheless, he should never dig her up after she is dead.

FUNNY BUSINESS!

I remember one of my pals from our days in the 'hood. Melvin was a bit insane, but generally a stand-up kind of guy. He was immensely gregarious and delighted in telling the most absurd stories. He was really quite funny for a comedian. It will surprise no-one to learn that that he was Jewish.

My favorite comedians are all Jewish and the list is incredible – Woody Allen, Jerry Seinfeld, Bette Midler, Ben Stiller, Whoopi Goldberg, Jerry Lewis, Mel Brooks, Billy Crystal and Gene Wilder.

The Jewish people I know today aren't that funny. Not that this is a criticism in any way. Life has been hard for many of them. There is my doctor, my insurance broker and the people who sell me my Sunday morning bagels. I must not forget one of the local restaurateurs. She could be funny if she wasn't so pushy. When I ordered an inexpensive local brew with my meal, she exclaimed "What, you don't want the Heineken?"

One of my advertising clients who really needed a sense of humor was Lou Stein. Lou had one of those beer and kraut places in the Adelaide Hills. The local population was made up of retired Westralians, Westphalians and the Wermacht. He was living in a demographic nightmare. Occasionally, Aryan customers would drift in but when they spied those lotto numbers on his arm, the bar was cleared and Lou was left lamenting. He was the only man in town who could get his beer wholesale, but he couldn't sell any.

I had this terrific campaign idea but Lou refused to change his name. Later, in deference to the West Australian mining magnate, he amended his Christian name to Lang and introduced Hancock's Happy Hour. Then the news came through announcing the dock strike. Soon, Lang was the only guy in town with German beer and all the old prejudices were soon forgotten. He put on a sausage sizzle with his cousin, Porky Grillstein, in charge of the barbecue. The McSteins were there. So were the O'Steins. Spud Murphy found that he had something in common with Pom Fritz and the place was filled with Helgas, Olgas, Gunters, Kurts and at least fifty-seven varieties of Heinz. It was good old Lang Stein and it wasn't even New Year.

I then decided to return to Melbourne. There were bigger mountains to climb than the Lou/Langs of this world but I knew that smart people would have their eye on Stein. This proved correct. His place became a magnet for all manner of luminaries and everyone wanted to be seen with Lou (he changed his name back after I left). There were photos of Sammy with Stein, Barbra and Stein, even Frank and Stein!

Lou tends bar to this day and continues one of Hahndorf's longest traditions. Whenever an empty barrel expires, the assembled patrons raise their empty glasses and shout in unison "Fill us Stein." Lou just laughs and untaps another keg.

Mel Brooks was the one who made us comfortable about being politically incorrect. Who else could have devised a musical about Hitler? Or the tale of an impresario who services old ladies in exchange for seed capital! Less gifted promoters would have surely baulked at the concept that was to become *The Producers* but this was grist to the mill for Mel and I think I understand why. He is probably mentally unbalanced. This isn't such a bad thing for a comedian. I suspect that Jim Carrey is out to lunch and poor Woody is a psychiatrist's dream. Only Seinfeld remains at peace with the world and his anecdotal routines are usually inoffensive. By George, it's amazing how a few zillion dollars can give you peace of mind.

COWBOYS!

I have a friend who is a trivia nut. He requires that I name *The Magnificent Seven* at least once a month. This request often comes via a telephone call from anywhere in the world. Even with such a regular memory jog, rarely do I score above five. Perhaps I don't care enough. After all, *M7* was just an exercise in gratuitous gunplay. I feel more at home with the thinking man's western, *High Noon*. When those two men faced off against each other, the tension and anticipation rippled through my sensory glands like the Michelin Man skating on thin ice.

The thing about cowboy movies is that you always get bang for your buck. The folks out west were always rootin', tootin' and shootin' and I liked that, even though this particular youngster had no idea what rootin' and tootin' meant. I thought that the wimmen were in the film for window dressing. The smart producers knew their target audience and there was no way that they would confuse a ten-year-old with a romantic plot. When I was that age, nubile Natasha from next-door used to flash her eyelashes at me, but my interest was down the road. Every Saturday afternoon, at the Odeon Theater, there would be a man with a gun. And he knew how to use it.

As one matured, those horrible cinema historians ruined it for us all. Did we really want to know that Buffalo Bill was a runt? Or that they reduced the size of the doorways to make him look bigger? There was worse to come. It appears that most of my heroes were gay, bisexual or vegetarian, which begs the point: Why bother with all that cattle rustling? They should have concentrated on the Indians.

There were two Red Indians that I remember very well: Cochise and....C'Mon! What was the name of the other one? Geronimo! I've got it. It was Sitting Bull. This is the gentleman who gave General Custer his last haircut and today, he still has a descendant living in the mid-west. His name is Couch-Potato and I know that he must be in pain every time he sees a repeat screening of one of those westerns. The Indians never won. Mind you, the opposition was formidable. Davy Crockett and Jim Bowie were good scouts and that Hopalong Cassidy, with his silver pistols, was a tribute to his wardrobe mistress. He was even color coordinated with his horse.

Because so many stories were based on actual events, you just can't discount them as irrelevant. It is true that the real Butch Cassidy didn't have Paul Newman's blue eyes and that the Sundance Kid couldn't dance, much less ride a bicycle. Pretty much everything else was true. Pat Garrett provided Billy the Kid with his just desserts and Doc Holliday and Wyatt Earp were excellent at the O.K. Corral. The authenticity of the singing cowboy is a little more dubious. I find it hard to believe that the very moral Gene Autry, son of a Methodist minister, would have ever found time to visit the Crazy Horse Saloon. This was the haven of outlaws, gunslingers and avowed bachelors who liked show tunes.

Nevertheless, you had to be impressed by his Cowboy Code, which was introduced to help budding caballeros come to terms with life in the saddle. He maintained that the cowboy was a patriot and must never shoot first, hit a smaller man or take unfair advantage. He must never go back on his word or a trust confided in him. He must always tell the truth. Wow! I could have been a contender.

Red River, the Yellow River, the River of no Return: the last frontier has been reached and all the stories have dried up. That is why a whole new generation of ten-year-old boys has been fed all this hocus-pocus Harry Potter rubbish, instead of gritty, old-fashioned cowboy magic. If they could see only half of what I've forgotten! Now, what were those last two names of *The Magnificent Seven?*

– VII –

SPORTING DELIBERATIONS!

Harry the Horse!

Focus!

Winners and Losers!

I don't like participating in sports in which they throw things at you. Baseball, cricket, tennis and boxing come immediately to mind. My father encouraged me to embrace the outdoors and one day, he put a strange looking implement in my hand. It was called a golf club and it would do until the real thing came along.

The marriage of sport and money is an engaging concept and it has fascinated me for years. There are people who maintain that horse racing is not really a sport but what do they know? The odds are never in your favor but you always have great expectations. What more can you ask from life than that?

HARRY THE HORSE!

I first became aware of Harry the Horse when I was seven years of age. He was an oddball character in a musical entertainment that had come to town and it was a real treat for me, because this was the only theater event that my pop had ever attended. It was a Saturday matinee and coincided with the cancellation of the day's events at the track due to inclement weather. His confreres

were a strange lot. Most were wearing pork-pie hats and each had a rolled up newspaper in their hand or one that was protruding from their pocket. Mistakenly, I presumed that they had brought their own toilet accessories to the theater. In those days, we all had an outside latrine and that was an appropriate use for the daily news.

The oddball characters didn't stop with Harry. There was Nicely, Nicely Johnson, Dave the Dude and Nathan Detroit: all regulars at the Saratoga racetrack and forever immortalized by Damon Runyon in his newspaper column, *Guys & Dolls*! I even shared their pain and disappointment when they were unable to conduct their illegal gambling at their regular spot behind the police station.

On that cold day, many years ago, I was to meet professional gamblers for the first time. Not that all of them were involved in a game of chance. Some of them were bookmakers. I had never been to a race meeting but I was familiar with the hovering presence at the bottom of our lane every Saturday. If mom was aware that dad had a gambling habit she didn't let on. As an older person, she would have known about bladder disorders and the like, but not me. I couldn't understand why our beloved bread-winner kept making those visits to the can every thirty minutes. Longer if there was a protest!

I attended my first race meeting a few years later. The frenetic invitations of the competing bookmakers cascaded over the milling throng, as punters scrambled over each other to try and acquire the best price. As I silently looked on, my hand automatically went to my breast pocket. Three recently ironed bills were about to discover what a rough world it is out there. These were the proceeds from my six months on the newspaper round and I was amazed that I had the willpower to blow it all in less than two minutes of anticipation, angst, aggravation and regret. The adrenalin associated with a successful photo finish result would come much later.

You might wonder how a small boy would be allowed onto a race course, unescorted. Over time, I acquired a few artificial uncles from amongst the regulars and usually slipstreamed in on their coattails. In later years, my real uncle was to become a confidante. While my pretentious relatives droned on about Renoir, Monet and the French masters, we discoursed on everything from the Breeder's Cup to the Melbourne Cup. Let's face it. Everyone knew that Greg Norman won the French Masters.

Losing Uncle Tom was a great shock. The man maintained a cabin up in the high country where he operated many betting accounts. His preferred bookie was Al Packer, who he called The Goat. I recall the Gorilla ($1,000) going on the 6/4 favorite, in a field of five and the magnificent beast saluted by eight lengths. Thankfully, I might add, because when he lost, there was Al to pay.

Tom was pretty excited until the jockey weighed in light and the horse was disqualified. To say that the mountain man was flabbergasted is an understatement. He had a heart attack and expired on the spot. Bookmakers came from everywhere to try and resuscitate him and I think it was uncharitable that some people would suggest that they were only trying to protect a guaranteed income stream.

My late uncle always asserted that bookies were a very generous bunch of people. He always scored a spot over the odds and if you were a pretty lass with a good bod, you could do even better than that. Not that there is ever any real chance of losing when taking wagers from women. They like to bet on omens, astrology numbers, birthdays and the color of the horse.

I was recently asked to write a tribute to bookmakers and you are now reading it. Can you believe that they no longer give me a spot over the odds? I still love them. At a time when monopolies and corporate decision-makers are taking all the fun out of our industry, we should appreciate their historical significance and cherish them for what they are. Bookmaking can be a very stressful occupation and so can punting. When my dad became a little recalcitrant with his debt repayment, our whole family had to leave the country, until things cooled down. We ended up with a Taco Bell franchise in Tennessee. I suppose you could say that things didn't really cool down.

As you might imagine, gambling became a rather touchy subject in our household. My sister, the nun, saw my repeated presence at the track as not only sinful but foolhardy. I could only agree but chose to take the Oscar Wilde perspective; it is better to repent a sin than regret the loss of a pleasure.

FOCUS!

I can't recall too many philosophical gems that I carried from childhood into adultery. However, I do remember one – "As you travel through life, always keep your eye upon the donut and not upon the hole." I don't know to whom to attribute this little masterpiece but I think they had a donut business. It certainly wasn't any weight watching organization that I know and I expect that professional golfers don't spend much time in bakeries.

It was my own father who introduced me to this noble game. He had just been appointed a trustee for a local club and presented me with a set of clubs that proudly bore the imprimatur from the Royal and Ancient home of golf. Evidently, he had bartered them for a bottle of scotch and I was impressed. If I knew then what I know now, I would have suggested that he keep the whisky. If you ever want to know whether you are capable of truly malicious acts, take up golf. I have wrapped my clubs around trees, thrown them into lakes, decapitated a passing duck and desecrated the memory of the holy family and all twelve apostles. I would have endured it all, if the good Lord had deemed fit to allow me just a single hole-in-one.

Obviously, there is some hostility there which is probably due to my verbal assaults on family and friends! Because of such profanity, there would only be a few golfers in heaven. It would be a tight list. Golf is not blessed with divine patronage but it does have its anointed ones. St Nick (aka Santa Claus) was a single handicap player, although he usually registered under his earthly alias, Jack Nicklaus.

Most of us struggle to play to our handicap. There are others who play golf below par. This is a rather contradictory term which means they play well. Even for the professionals, competition is fierce and sometimes it can be a jungle out there. There are tigers, golden bears and even the odd snake in the grass. To wit, one Oric Goldfinger, who bent the rules in his match with James Bond, one of Scotland's finest players? In the days gone by, there were so many rules. Nobody knew how to police them, except those early champions, Bobby Jones and Bobby Locke. I won't even attempt to confuse you about the 19th hole. This is where you have some beers with your peers. Would you go to the bar if you hadn't scored a par? No way, Callaway!

What has this got to do with donuts, you may well ask? It's all about focus, my friend. Keep your eye on the ball and aim the ball at the hole. If you miss, you can blame the wind, the cut of the green or your mother-in-law. If somebody breaks wind when you are lining up the final hole at Augusta, you may be excused for any subsequent retribution. If you are new to this pastime, there are two ways of looking at it. It is a whole new ball game or a ball game full of holes! Either way, there is still time to bail out and retain your sanity.

Now that I have almost finished this particularly probing profile and have anguished over the philosophical aspects of my shallow life, I remember where I first came across these words of wisdom. This definitive dab of doggerel didn't come from Lord Byron, Molière, Shakespeare or even William Shatner. It came from the sixteen-year-old kid who worked the jam donut stand outside Yankee Stadium. He also did Chinese Fortune Cookies, Fantale wrappers and football cards. Today, he is the chief executive officer of a multinational

The IRA Annual Golf Tournament

greeting card firm. You can certainly go a long way with a bit of bullshit. Believe me, I know.

WINNERS AND LOSERS!

Recently, I caught up with some Greek history on the telly and I have to say that Achilles was a real heel. After slaying the fearless Hector, he tied him to the back of his chariot and let loose around the public arena in an arrogant display of self glorification. Those titans of Troy, who were having a pita on the piazza, nearly gagged on their kebabs. Official records of this event indicate that the terribly talented and tastefully tanned Paris successfully obtained revenge with a skillfully directed projectile. Ah, the slings and arrows of Greek Mythology!

I was surprised to learn that an arrow in the ankle could be terminal. Today, with the advances in medical science, it would be no more deadly than an anterior cruciate injury, which our own gladiators suffer regularly in the sporting arena. Not only did I shamelessly sit through these endless scenes of brutality but I couldn't help but wish I was there. Not for the fighting, mind you. It's just that they didn't seem to have any bookmakers working the battle. When they wheeled in that Trojan horse, there was only ever going to be one winner and I would have loved to be there for the kill.

Betting on a one-horse race can be disconcerting. Especially if you don't know which nag is the ring-in. For the people of Troy, there was really only one horse to consider and they still screwed it up. Wooden-heads! When Steven Bradbury won that gold medal at odds of one thousand to one, who would have guessed that the other competitors would all fall over? Just the punter who put acid on the laces of their ice skates!

I think that we could all be guilty of insider trading if we had the opportunity. This brings me to boxing. They say that you're going to fight in a ring which is square. It is also a man's sport but the prize is a purse. Then you get belted. You get belted in the face, in the stomach, below the belt, above the belt and then, when you win the championship, they give you another belt. If you want to bet, you have to take on the fat guy with the cigar and the two bodyguards. He takes your money and gives you his marker. You have this feeling that you'll never see him again. When you discover him bonding with the referee, it's time to call a cab.

People with clout and inside information are recognized by their perfectly groomed fingernails. They don't have worries. If one has a perceived advantage, you can always enter a contest with confidence and a degree of smugness. Only bad luck, trickery or gross dishonesty from your competitor will foil your endeavors. There is nothing worse than being outgunned by someone who is more dishonest than you are. When Chicago mobster Al Capone came to town for the Saratoga races in New York, he always used to take the jockeys out to lunch the day before the big event. Unfortunately, on one of these occasions, the hoops had just come from a breakfast meeting with local identity Lucky Luciano. He wasn't called Lucky for nothing, so they were put in an invidious position and were understandably nervous about the outcome.

To this day, that Saratoga race is unequalled in its infamy. Nine of the ten jockeys fell off just after the start but retribution was avoided when those operating the tote windows gladly paid out to Al, even though his horse failed to complete the course. All of the fallen jockeys put their bad luck down to food poisoning. It is pretty hard to win at the best of times. When you factor in impenetrables, such as dirty rotten scoundrels, the odds become longer by the minute. I have friends who scoff at my fixation with gambling but they have no understanding of the joy of pain. Only committed punters will understand the anguish and agony associated with a roulette ball that rolls one number too far.

If you only take fifty dollars to the track, that's all you've lost. Everything else is pure entertainment. The atmosphere, the anticipation, the camaraderie of good friends! If you meet Hector, Helen, Troy or Paris at the Souvlaki Bar, don't take any tips from them. They're not really into horses.

– VIII –

OLD BLIGHTY!

The man that I could have been!

The man in the silk pajamas!

London! It is every Australian's first big adventure. You save for years to get there and when you do, you complain about everything from their warm beer to their ghastly weather. If only the Brits were pleased to see you but they're not. When they sent us off to the antipodes in those convict ships, they never really thought that we would come back. The jobs are scarce and you take what you can get. In the interim, one must make the time-honored pilgrimage to *Oktoberfest* and any other beer festival that might be geographically possible.

Your nearest and dearest don't realize that you are doing it tough and there is no way that you are going to fess up to such an embarrassing state of affairs. So, you make up a load of rubbish and send them the news in a letter, without a stamp. I know that I did.

THE MAN THAT I COULD HAVE BEEN!

People often ask me what I do. They think I do nothing. These are the same people that believe my employer, Universal Exports, runs a one man show. In fact, there are two of us.

While 007 gadflies around the globe, avoiding deadly tarantula spiders, bikini-clad assassins and crotch-probing lasers, I stay at home to clean up his mess, which is quite considerable. You may be aware that catastrophic explosions seem to generate themselves whenever James is nearby and acceptance of these urban disasters is only tolerated because of skilful diplomacy by representatives of the Crown. Immediate reparation is expected.

My list for last year included five surface-to-air missiles, two nuclear power plants, an oil rig and a space satellite. Bond also lost the Hope diamond and his invisible Aston Martin. He couldn't find it. I don't mind the paperwork. There are always impact studies of some kind; plus environmental trauma reports and survivor statements. What I am dirty about are the budget cuts that are usually passed down after his big day out. While Golden Boy subjects his finely tuned body to a diet of canapés and aperitifs, I'm riding the reality trail. You won't find Beluga caviar or a Vodka Martini in the Bat Cave. Just tepid tea, stirred not shaken and a discount digestive, dunked not crunched.

You may think that I fulfill an important function in the global world of espionage and political intrigue. No one else does. In fact, I am sure that Universal Exports is a very small player in the scale of things. My only contacts with the bureaucracy are two people called Q and M. If we were important, A, B or C would come around occasionally. One person who does make his presence felt is Mr T, the tax man. Even James Bond has to submit an annual return and you can guess which bunny has to prepare it. Some time ago, I decided not to file under the International Playboy category and positioned our hero as a specialist in pest eradication. This gave us substantial deductions on workplace expenses such as waterproof tuxedos, condoms, gambling chips and state-of-the-art weaponry.

If he needs time off to play in the World Cup, the Olympic Fencing Championships or the Spies Slalom Shoot-out, I usually grasp the opportunity to take some of my own well-earned leave. I always tell people that Margate and Blackpool are just as exciting as ever and why wouldn't I? These truly British summer retreats are a world away from the MI6 time-share retirement village in Benidorm. Ah, the big R word! Should I have mentioned it? Was it 1962 when James first locked horns with Dr No and the delectable Honey Ryder? He seems to get younger with every passing year and I suspect he deducts a year with every birthday. I seem to be growing old, alone.

Organizations like SPECTRE and SMERSH don't need retirement plans because their agents are always killed off in the line of duty. You know who works on the assumption that you only live twice, so he goes and gets himself cremated. How can you top that?

There are a lot of occupational hazards in our line of work and you have to be fairly sprightly to dodge a mad Russian, with a poisoned knife in her shoe. Sure, there are superficial wounds to be had but the real killers are stress and prostate complaints. Thank goodness for National Health. If you have a license to thrill, you get a goldfinger up your ass. The rest of us just get a cold finger. Commander Bond also has a liver problem, which would surprise no one. All that French champagne and vintage brandy can't be good for you. Of course, like most fair-minded people, I abhor ambitious megalomaniacs with dreams of world domination and there is only one man with the budget to stop them. This is where Moneypenny comes in. You don't think that he would be fawning all over her unless she had the keys to the mint in her chastity belt, do you? Our man from Special Branch always travels first class and that's how it should be. What about me, you ask? Well, as long as the 6.15 pm to Clapham Junction arrives on time, I'll live to die another day.

Happy in the service!

I had always wanted to work for the secret service. The only downside was their demand for anonymity when working undercover. If you can't wear your distinguished service medal at your local bar, how do you get to pick up chicks? I was in no way a navy seal and I don't like water all that much. I wouldn't envy the prospect of a confrontation with an octopus, a manta ray or a squad of underwater subversives carrying spear-guns. The gambling bit I can take. I am a dab hand at chemin de fer and other games of chance and with the government picking up the tab, you can't lose. You meet a better class of person in the high roller's room, the munchies are more imaginative and the booze is usually free. If I don't mind saying so, I can also look deceptively suave in a tux, with a Walther PPK tucked under my left arm.

When you first look over the application form, you immediately have your doubts. It is always difficult to know whether you would be suited to a job like this. There is a lot of travel involved and you need to be available for cocktail parties on yachts, massages, lobster dinners and the occasional André Rieu concert. It is all part of your cover and this is necessary because criminal figures with high intelligence only operate out of exotic locations. Prior to service, I had always been a fan of James Bond and I must admit that much of this adulation was based on envy. His apparent rapport with supermodels and other beautiful people is far removed from my tentative efforts at seduction. I was once rejected by a relief worker at the Sperm Bank and never got over it.

I realize that in real life, the average Joe is not likely to come up against the likes of the KGB or the despicable Ernst Blofeld. Nevertheless, the man from MI6 can be a role model for us all because his personal attributes are without reproach. Not only is this fellow a walking encyclopedia but his knowledge of vintage wines and Fabergé eggs has saved his bacon on more than one occasion. Do you remember that arch-villain who blew his cover to 007 when he ordered red wine with fish?

Sometimes, treachery can be a money thing but government service never is. Any public servant will tell you that. You put it all on the line for Queen and country and I'm pretty happy with that kind of commitment. For years, people have been telling me that I am a big zero, so it's not a big transition to a double zero number and a license to kill. If one has to quaff a bit of champagne and bed a few bimbos in the line of duty, that's OK too.

Some of my friends poured scorn on me and my desire to become an agent provocateur, because they didn't think I would be good at it. "How would you be able to seduce a supermodel?" they said. "You don't know anything" was the general consensus. Certainly, I didn't fare well in the oral examination that they set for me. Evidently, the *Mannekin Pis* is in Brussels and not in the Ralph Lauren restroom that I had nominated.

Not everyone will be as stylish, sophisticated and charismatic as I am and many will have trouble with the entrance exam. You know that they won't let you take your puppy with you on jobs, don't you? These are heartless people but they have to be. Confident, scheming individuals, with ambitious plans for world domination are everywhere. Some of them have even mastered Sudoku.

It is always difficult to overcome your insecurities in order to become a superior person and I sympathize with those of you who have grappled with the certainty of truth and come up short of the mark. Nevertheless, a journey of a thousand miles starts with a single step. My friend Felix is currently running a *Crime and Punishment Guided Tour*, which is proving very popular. For a very reasonable cost, you can be tortured in the Kremlin, mangled in the Tower of London and do solitary confinement at Alcatraz. Why don't you just go out and enjoy yourself and leave the hard stuff to me?

THE MAN IN THE SILK PAJAMAS!

I had always wanted to meet Hugh Hefner. Most children like to take a teddy bear to bed with them. I always opted for a bunny and as I got older, little happened to change my mindset.

A bunch of us were in the Playboy Club in London. It was the swinging seventies and I had a real live breathing bunny sitting on my lap. It was an exhilarating experience. When I say that she was breathing, this is a slight exaggeration. Because she was tucked so tightly into her skimpy costume, she was making a kind of breathless gasping sound, which I had misinterpreted as celebrity panting. I had put it about that I was Madonna's current beau and looking for some talent to star in my new epic, entitled *In Bed with Three Playboy Bunnies*. The word got back to Hefner and it wasn't long before he was online, long distance from LA. He felt that he had the credentials to go on the payroll as an official advisor and was expecting such an invitation. He also indicated that there were some copyright issues and that I may wish to come over and visit at the Playboy Mansion.

People of my vintage will shudder with delight when they recall the reported shenanigans that went on at Hugh's medieval castle in the Hollywood Hills during the seventies. It was one continuous party with babes, booze and general urban debauchery. Not that there's anything wrong with that! The prospect of an entrée into this kind of lifestyle filled me with gleeful anticipation but there was a small problem concerning my own credentials. I was hoping that he wasn't a good friend of Madonna's.

Hef had me picked up at the airport and you have to be impressed by his style. Somehow, he had learnt that I was a free-wheeler and even knew my birth date. Miss July was waiting for me. I was impressed by her skills on "the Hog" and there was no better judge. Only a few days earlier, I had been a courier in old London town. Now I was a movie producer.

I had always been amused by the fact that the man was always interviewed in pajamas or a robe. There was a casting couch in nearly every room and I soon realized that he never had time to get dressed. Undressing was never a problem. On that first night, we chewed the fat and I found him very amusing, entertaining and enthusiastic about my film. He found me vague and evasive and probably wondered why my answers were completely devoid of any detail concerning the project. When he was called away, I presumed that I would have the run of the playroom and the liquor cabinet. As it turned out, all the girls had an early curfew and alcohol was banned on Wednesdays. However, card and board games were available. Damn!

I never saw Hef again. The next morning, I found my bags packed and placed on the front porch. A battered taxi arrived soon after, manned by a toothless Mexican, with a distasteful after-smell. I was whisked away to the airport terminal and a few days later I was sitting back on my own wheels in the West End. I sometimes look back at those days and wonder what might have been. My conduct during those forgotten years was reprehensible. I've moved on. So has my G spot. It has repositioned itself, approximately six inches north. These days, someone can get me going with a half-decent mushroom risotto. Not that I don't pine for the occasional rabbit pie.

– IX –

EMERALD ISLE!

The Tourist!

I have one remaining Irish relative, who lives in the shadows of Slievenamon, a highly respected mountain range in County Tipperary. He is a bit shell-shocked. His home village was officially named "the most boring town in Ireland." On top of that, my late aunt steadfastly refused to acknowledge the ties that bind because there was a drinking problem in the family, some two hundred years earlier. After her demise, I rifled through her stock portfolio and was astounded to find substantial share certificates issued by the Guinness Brewery. Of course, she may have had them for two hundred years.

It is common knowledge that some of my jobs in London were highly classified. Others were not. My stint in advertising coincided with the IRA bomb season and I must admit that this did make me feel uncomfortable. I then came up with the bright idea that I might be safer over there. So, I claimed some leave and became a tourist.

THE TOURIST!

The Irish are a nation of friendly, warm and hospitable people. They wouldn't dream of offending you and are even predisposed to getting a laugh at their own expense. One of their most popular raconteurs takes great delight in explaining that Ireland is an island, three hundred miles long and two hundred miles thick. I was the perennial tourist, with a hired compact to prove it. It was cute and minute but I didn't know how to reverse the car and was too embarrassed to ask. They might ask how thick Australia is.

Getting directions in Ireland can sometimes be a problem. They always tell you that you are starting from the wrong place. I can get very excited, listening to one of those sublime brogues, redolent of Dublin and the southern counties but, this time, I decided to wing it. A map was available from the McDonald's franchise, at the airport, listing a dozen restaurants with golden arches that I might encounter en route to the city. You may think that this is a large number for such a short journey but one should realize that the potato is very much the staple diet in this part of the world.

I was looking forward to my first Guinness, which you may have heard, is made from the tears of angels. I don't know who was responsible for the waterworks outside the hotel but O'Connell St. had been crying all afternoon. The locals have about two dozen ways to describe a rainy day and they are all complimentary. But, would you really need to go outside? The conviviality of the Irish pub offers so much: a pint of porter, some genuine blarney, a few pretty colleens and a small fiddle band. Heaven is where you find it.

It was hard to leave Dublin. The Hurling Final at Croke Park is a must for all sports fans and I had been keen to take in this intriguing but rather hostile conflict. I can recall my father describing the game as being ten per cent safer than war. A little further south, the Curragh of Kildare is acres of beautiful, rolling plains and the historical home of the Irish thoroughbred. A national treasure, the thoroughbred horse in Ireland is high on the pecking order, alongside bloodstained patriots, sozzled playwrights and off-key musicians. All would have attended the Irish Derby at The Curragh at some stage during their march to glory.

Unfortunately, I was unable to adjust my program as I was committed to attending the matchmaking festival in the west coast village of Lisdoonvarna. This spa town invigorates itself every year with this quaint homage to love lost. Who was it who said "It is better to have loved and lost than to never have loved at all?" On reflection, it was a Frankie Laine melody from years gone by. To my mind, some of the prospective lovers were well past their use-by date. They would definitely remember Frank when he was a Frankie.

To help with the introductions, official matchmakers will investigate the respective qualities of both the sexes. If you need to take a spinster for a spin, one of these facilitators will arrange to hire a dilapidated coupe from a neighbor, who, invariably, will be a relative. If nothing works out, it is not a lost week. There are many associated activities, culminating with the picnic race meeting, where you should be alert but not alarmed. Sometimes, the third race starts before the second. I managed to leave Lisdoornvarna in an unbetrothed state, which was a sad reflection on the efforts of the matchmakers. Especially as my hair didn't come off with my hat! This is usually a good sign.

It was another soft day when I urged my little car south in the direction of Limerick, located in an area called Munster. The Americans made a television series about a rather dysfunctional family called *The Munsters* but I was assured that there was no connection. I was asked to concentrate on the stunning spectacle that was soon to appear: Killarney. I'm glad that I did. Forever immortalized in musical anthology, the blue waters of the Killarney Lakes are unblemished perfection and everything you would want them to be. From there, one of Ireland's most traveled tourist routes awaits: the Ring of Kerry. With God on your right and Dingle Bay on your left, all you need is a friendly bed and breakfast to break the journey. You'll find that alright.

It had been my intention to investigate the extent of the blarney in Killarney and the local public houses are ideally placed to provide the tourist with the kind of colloquial awakening that can't be promoted in the travel brochures. The real Blarney Stone is in Cork and if you kiss it, you are blessed with eternal eloquence. I wonder what happens if you sit on it?

One of the delights of this part of Ireland is the seaside town of Kinsale, a charming fishing village of historical significance and one of the oldest and most important outposts of the early Gaelic aristocracy. Today, it boasts many fine restaurants and every October hosts a gourmet festival that attracts tourists from near and far. Expect great fishing and fabulous pubs. To say that the atmosphere is always convivial is an understatement. Some years ago, I attended an advertising convention in this very town, which included a contingent of some eighty people from Finland. We found out later that none of them were in the advertising business.

It will be no surprise to learn that my little car had opted for another spectacular coastal journey past Ballycotton en route to Waterford where they make the finest crystal in the world. I was dead keen to meet a glass-blower with the hiccups. Every major sporting trophy in existence must come from this factory. They create two of everything, just in case. As a child, I certainly loved breaking crystal glasses. That's why my mother banned me from the kitchen sink for life (and they said that I wasn't smart enough to get into Mensa).

Onwards to Tipperary! As I navigated myself through the hump on the horizon that is known as the Knockmealdown Mountains, I reflected on my grandfather's graphic memories of John L. Sullivan and his bare knuckle predecessors. One could surely buy himself a fight around here. Coming up next was Slievenamon, another mountain and a lyrical feast for countless balladeers and warblers of traditional music.

As I meandered through Killenaule, Balingarry and Kilkenny, the car radio locked onto the country and western hour and Johnny Cash started gargling-on about the forty shades of green. The vistas were indeed lush and thank goodness for the compact. The trees were completely arched over the small winding road, as if this was my own personal carriageway into heaven. It nearly was, when a recalcitrant tractor made an unscheduled stop, just inches in front of my bumper.

The small town of Avoca looked very familiar and I soon realized why. *Ballykissangel* souvenirs were abundant and the Catholic priest was doing autograph sessions after mass. The Wicklow Mountains were the stuff of dreams but unfortunately the dream was over. I was due back across the water to source some music for our major client's fashion parade. Of course, I had already done it. Could there be anything more appropriate than *Danny Boy* for a London derrière?

– X –

LAND OF OPPORTUNITY!

All-American Boy!

The girl in the tight blouse!

One day at a time!

If you have stars in your eyes, you have to go to America. That is why it was my dear old star-struck mom who was the catalyst for our first family visit. My sister was baptized Beverley Burke because our maternal protector thought that this was a name that would look good in lights. After Beverley joined the convent, it was down me to make some sort of creative statement.

I am usually quite good at making statements but I regret that I chose to lecture the President on his managerial skills. Nobody liked me after that and with good reason. I was a terrible name dropper and you could never believe a word that I said. In Hollywood, you would have thought that would be enough to get my name in lights.

ALL-AMERICAN BOY!

I was just fourteen years old when I started delivering for Taco Bell. My old man was the manager and it was a 24/7 franchise, mainly due to the repeat business from Graceland. I had been to the mansion about a dozen times but never set eyes on the great man. Early one morning, the call came. It was a single order of enchiladas, tortillas, frijoles, tacos, a breakfast burrito and double fries. Also, a lo-cal Dr Pepper for Priscilla! It was now or never.

I found Elvis in the kitchen with his hound dog who was there for the scraps. I don't know if you have a mutt who likes Mexican but I can tell you that the air is never fresh. It didn't bother "the King" one bit and I was impressed with his humor, humility and total generosity of spirit. He was fascinated by my accent and we swapped stories until the sun came up. There were to be many dawn breakfasts like this and we found common ground on many levels. He liked jelly donuts. So did I. We both wore blue suede shoes. It was as if we were on a parallel plane on a journey to infinity. When Jerry Lee Lewis announced that he was going to marry his 13 year old cousin, we just looked at each other with suspicious minds. Could you blame us? Sometimes, remnants of the band would still be in the house after an all-night music session. These early-morning jamborees were never popular with the neighbors. Once, the sheriff arrived and arrested everybody although light-heartedly.

The warden threw a party in the county jail. Autographs were signed and everyone was home within twenty-four hours. How could you object to people like Elvis and the Jordanaires? People often ask me whether I noticed his physical decline and if so, why didn't I do something about it? In truth, I never knew whether it was down to his junk food, pill-popping or bad acting. My pop had a financial investment in the former indiscretion, so I decided that the practical thing to do was to say nothing. He didn't look good when he departed for his last big concert in Hawaii. Because I screwed up the time difference, I only tuned in after Elvis had left the building. I could imagine the stretch limo trolling the streets of Honolulu, looking for hot tamales and chili dogs. Not long after this, I moved on from the fast-food industry and into the publishing world.

Elvis also checked out. Dead at forty-two! I do miss him because he really was my mentor. When no-one else could understand me! When everything I did was wrong! He was always there with that big cheesy grin and picadillo or mole sauce dribbling down his chin. Pardon me if I'm sentimental but for many of us, Memphis, Tennessee has never been the same. The big house is now a museum and the memory lives on. However, without the physical presence, those chairs in his parlor seem empty and bare.

I know that Elvis is probably still playing guitar and leading a heavenly chorus but I bet he still yearns to be in that land of cotton; old times there are not forgotten. I wish I was in Dixie myself. So much so, I have even applied for the position of CEO, Taco Bell, which has just become available. I gave the letter to the postman and he put it in his sack.

THE GIRL IN
THE TIGHT BLOUSE!

Those North American waterways can be quite treacherous. I was in the front stalls of the Odeon Theater when Bob Mitcham and Marilyn Monroe confronted some pretty belligerent rapids in their homemade raft. The film was *River of No Return* and the blonde bombshell in the tight blouse was thrown into the water with great regularity. My fellow truants unanimously agreed that she should take off her shirt. Otherwise, she would end up with a death of a cold. Unfortunately, the censors were disagreeable people and all we got was a portent of things to come: the wet T-shirt!

I was too young to know Marilyn in the old days. She had progressed from Miss California Artichoke Queen to be the inaugural cover girl for Playboy magazine. That famous nude calendar was big news and wasn't she a tease? When the charismatic sex symbol told those gossip columnists that she had nothing on but the radio, they melted in the afterglow of her complete candor. As a calendar girl, she fielded many offers and requests for product endorsements, most of which she refused. A confectionary company wanted to name an ice cream after her but she thought that this was in bad taste. Anyway, she was hot property and everyone knew it. Marilyn cultivated her breathless diction to such an extent that many people thought that she suffered from Asthma. I can think of no other reason for the universal fascination with her chest.

Not long after I arrived in Hollywood, I was writing lyrics for a Gorilla-Gram agency and who should walk in but Norma Jean? Her career was going well but she was keen to take some singing lessons. The boss shunted her into the tribute department and it wasn't long before she was singing "Happy Birthday" to anybody who was anybody. Apart from her JFK performance, she also warbled "Many Happy Returns" for people like Jimmy Hoffa, Sam Cooke and Martin Luther King.

My own musical ability was rather limited but nobody expected much from a Gorilla. However, I could play the spoons and my tap dancing was above average. For some reason, we hit it off famously and it wasn't long before Marilyn was introducing me as the boy wonder from down-under. In those days, if you did a reading for a Batman episode, you never lived it down.

We used to hang out together after my gigs and everybody wanted to know about the guy in the monkey suit. There was talk that I might be considered for a part in the remake of *King Kong*. They actually wanted to send me to Hong Kong. Marilyn was the centre of the universe and studio control was an accepted part of life in Hollywood. But she didn't want to be manipulated. Her continual assignations with Arthur Miller surprised many, including myself. His writing credits were impressive but he looked like Clark Kent on acid.

This wasn't good news for the spin doctors, who were already fighting Monroe's desire to be accepted as a serious actress. I remember talking to Lee Strasberg, at the Actor's Studio, about this. He doesn't. He thought that I was bringing him coffee. Nevertheless, he was an important person in her life and few people would know that he was the main beneficiary in her will. She didn't let him down but others were less than impressed. Marilyn was totally unreliable and always late for work. Some people were saying that she was getting her work ethic from me. Balls! I blame the politicians and you know who I am talking about. Since her death, many have chosen to perpetuate her memory but she wasn't a candle in the wind and diamonds weren't her best friend. I was. She just didn't know it.

ONE DAY AT A TIME!

I have always thought that I would make a good State Governor. Perhaps even President! That is why I have some empathy with the new Commander in Chief and the challenges that lay ahead. Who else can provide him with the kind of considered advice that can only emanate from someone outside conventional political circles? I tried to slip my political manifesto under the door of the White House, just before the new man's first day in office. There was a slight hiccup and it now looks like he will have to wait for the mail delivery from Guantanamo Bay.

My Manifesto!

It is imperative that you start with a clean desk but it will be hard to ignore that large white envelope that they always leave on the blotter. This is the list of people to whom you owe favors and it is a long list. If you are smart, you will have lost track of the number of influential sympathizers, interest groups, apparatchiks and ideological confreres who have helped you on your political journey. They can't help you anymore. Burn the list.

Traditionally, one shunts a legitimate political competitor into the wilderness but you have taken a new tack and put her onto the world stage. While the Secretary of State is out of the country, you can have a lot of fun with the Treasury, re-determining the fiscal boundaries of the budget. It is never too early to kick-start your re-election campaign, so move those tax dollars around to your advantage. Don't worry about any voter backlash here. We are used to this kind of thing and realize that neither flood nor famine would interfere with a Polly's steely determination to get re-elected.

By now, your first morning in the job is nearly over and you are probably hungry. Go to lunch with no-one. They all want to get in your ear. Photos of the boss having a salad sandwich in the office always look good in the tabloids. These photo opportunities can be arranged with your secretary's Polaroid. You don't have to actually meet the press. Your first afternoon appointment should be with your travel agent. Which countries are ideal for bilateral discussions on anything? Departmental advisors will recommend trade delegations to only nations with sun and a beach. If you like one destination more than most, the sister city thing is a good way to go.

On both sides of politics, there have always been questions asked about jobs for the boys, travel junkets, unwise dalliances, public relations fiascos and alcohol-induced gaffes. If any of these issues roll over into your second week, just bluff them with your indifference. That you might be a bit of a rake would be appealing to certain members of the community, who would see you in their own image. The comparison may disgust you but they do vote and that is important. You can also raise your level of acceptability by embracing the Arts. Unfortunately, this is a one way street and involves continual hand-outs. If you can actually quote Shakespeare or converse, knowingly, about the brown-eyed belly dancers of Botswana, you are already ahead of the game. You will also meet lots of other chaps who know about mandates.

Some people will advise you to be brutal, rather than conciliatory and I endorse that. If those minorities block up the freeways with their rage, drop them in the Potomac River. The graffiti people will be just as happy doing rock sculptures in Folsom Prison. I have a lot of great ideas like this. That is why I think I would be good in the big chair. If you ignore all those smartasses who are trying to impose their will on you, the country will run itself.

There will always be a crisis of some magnitude. Whether it is law and order, a teacher revolt or a medical emergency, your media representative will be available to quote endless statistics which will confuse and infuriate. Being a wise leader and a great anticipator, you will be in Trinidad and Tobago, accepting a good neighbor award on behalf of the nation. The aggrieved just want more money, better working conditions or a ten hour week. Nothing unreasonable there! If you are back from the tropics in time to defuse the situation, remember not to use any big words like "promise" or "guarantee."

Those media microphones will be forever aimed at your larynx and it's not because you're good at karaoke.

Of course, harmony is everything as is loyalty. Your associates live for the day when they can hear you proclaim that they have your complete confidence. If you can do this with a straight face, you're really getting the hang of this job. Some of your people will be concerned with climbing the tree of succession but naked ambition is best left to the kingmakers in your party. For you, the Presidency should be one big party. If there are awkward questions about cash cows and other agricultural matters, just give them your best poker face. If you play your cards right, you can be boss for a long, long time. At least, until I am ready to take over!

That's me with the grey hair.

– XI –

FRIENDS AND ACQUAINTANCES!

A bad penny always turns up.

Bad habits die hard.

They say that you can't choose your relatives. Nevertheless, those with a prison address can be easily disowned or ignored. Recently, I have been reflecting on the friends and acquaintances that I have acquired over the years and I have come to the conclusion that I am continually surrounded by rascals, scallywags, layabouts and dodgy entrepreneurs. Of course, I love them dearly.

You may have noticed that the word "bad" appears in the title of both of the forthcoming articles. This is no more than poetic license and doesn't reflect on the character and moral fiber of the central characters. Who am I to denigrate or belittle their chosen profession?

A BAD PENNY
ALWAYS TURNS UP.

They say this because it is true. There are some individuals in my life whose mere presence gives off an emphatic aura that transposes me into a state of anxiety: people who can't exist without power or money! I have managed to survive this mortal coil without either and I believe that I am well-adjusted because of it. So, why am I so nervous in their company?

I can remember when all was well with the world. It was in the sixties at the Monterey Folk Festival in California. Actually, I don't remember much at all. There was Puff, the Magic Dragon and my Yankee friend Billy Gates who empowered me with his traditional support for justice and the American way. He was a bit of a nerd so I introduced him to a girl who had silicon implants. I thought that he would never notice. Evidently, they were very small but soft.

Bill was a nice guy with a million ideas. Open and honest! There are so many that aren't and they have the creative diligence and charisma to charm you right through their deception and beyond. When I purchased a twenty percent share of the Golden Gate Bridge for ten thousand dollars in 1969, my bête noire was a chap called Soapy Smith. This dude was a real slippery customer.

Don't you love them for their sheer audacity and self-belief? My man had more front than a rabbit with a gold tooth, but in the end, he bit off more than he could chew. Soapy was doing a sales pitch on the bridge at Chappaquiddick, when an errant vehicle knocked him into the channel below. His body was never recovered. Only at the memorial service did I get to meet his other victims. They were there to grieve and pay their respects to a true rogue. His family didn't turn up but I did hear on the grapevine that none of them answered to the surname "Smith."

His attorney provided the homily and the pallbearers looked like they had been recruited from the underbelly of American society. I prayed that I could remain both anonymous and insignificant. Unfortunately, I was recognized by another inmate from the school of hard knocks. His name was Angelo but everyone called him The Dip. In no time at all, his adventurous hand snaked around my shoulder and before the garlic aftermath of his last meal could render me senseless, I surreptitiously transferred my wallet to a more secure environment.

Like Soapy, Angelo was a product of his environment. They profited by the same legal representation but while my man had a clean slate, his friend's litany of misdemeanors and criminal flirtations was an ongoing worry for his poor widowed mother. I caught a glimpse of her rosary beads. They had depreciated at least five times the normal rate. I don't often get involved in another person's problems but I could tell that he was mixing with the wrong people. A hard-working lad but oblivious to all social responsibility! I didn't really expect him to know the IRS Commissioner by name but I was surprised that he was unaware of his actual role in our commercial society.

Am I too quick to call him a bad penny? Hitler was a bad penny. So was Al Capone and yet, he was very religious. In fact, he religiously terminated over one hundred people before he was twenty-one. He condoned this anti-social behavior by claiming that they had it coming. I suppose you have to respect that. The allure of the fast buck is a craving that we all must deal with. The corporate high flyers do it better than most. Call it a performance bonus if you like but they can drain a balance sheet like an elephant in a bathtub.

I really do miss the indelible personalities as typified by Soapy Smith and his ilk. If there was a Hall of Fame for personal deception and outrageous duplicity, he would stand alone. I was never nervous in his company and right now, I really could entertain the prospect of someone being able to turn a penny into a pound.

Update!

Having read the preceding potpourri of predicaments that symbolize the type of encounters that frequently materialize when I am let loose into the community, you will appreciate the fact that I have no screening process to protect me from those who might be considered devious and deceitful. I am not good at character assessment. Of more concern in these troubled times is my lazy attitude to financial investment but I am improving. In the old days, words like risk assessment and due diligence were not part of the vernacular. Now, when I am at the track or involved in an intense poker game, careful consideration is always the norm. If only it made a difference.

I am hopeful of surviving the financial crisis. I have heard that the traffic flow on the Golden Gate Bridge has improved considerably and my investment in the Mirage Casino and Hot Springs in the Gobi Desert is also looking good. I believe that we are negotiating with Kylie Minogue to perform at our opening extravaganza in 2020.

BAD HABITS DIE HARD.

Never let it be said that I was anything less than an attentive scholar during my formative years. Nevertheless, occasional truancy was always blessed relief from the daily dosage of Pythagoras. It was a measure of my confidence that I was always smug in my assertion that the last place one would expect to find me was in the betting ring, at one of the inner city racetracks. Ah, those wonderful Wednesdays!

One day, I ran into Fr O'Flaherty, the school bursar. Oops! The good father looked resplendent in an eye-level felt Fedora and high-collared trench coat. The absurdity of such an outfit during high summer was not lost on me. I imagine that this clandestine cleric was equally amused at my artificial measles spots which was my fall-back position should I get sprung. As I had never heard Fr O'Flaherty preach from the pulpit about the evils of gambling, I couldn't understand his desire for anonymity. Most bookmakers would gladly give a reverend gentleman a few points over the odds. It didn't even occur to me that there might be some nefarious association between the good thing in the fifth, a jittery Jesuit and his trusted position as keeper of the college purse.

As it turned out, there wasn't. He was just putting a few shekels on for the syndicate back at the rectory. Shackled by the burden of celibacy, there were few vices left that these sky-pilots could get enthusiastic about. Of course, if we knew then what we know now, but let's not get judgmental.

You can't go to the races without acquiring a few amigos. Fr Joe's sidekick was a very proficient gambler called Pete the Punter. A tall man, erect and proud, he towered above the panorama of pork-pies, trilbies, shiny domes and blue rinses. He was always in a state of perpetual inertia, which was a tribute to his concentration. There would be no dash for the best odds when the plunge was activated. Nor would there be any frantic reevaluation when the coat-tuggers arrived. As they always do. Pete was a professional. Cool, calm and collected! Which he did quite often! Not that he was aloof, mind you. The fact of the matter was that the appraisal had already been made and there would only be one bet that day. Perhaps Colin, the gregarious, might drop by.

"How ya doing, Pete? Backed any winners?" "I haven't had a bet" the placid punter would reply, knowing full well that he was only seconds away from meaningful eye contact with a well-known, commission agent.

For most bookies, happiness is a warm yuppie. There is very little challenge there. The professional is sane, sober and has done his homework. The salacious elements of his persona might emerge but this would be long after he has bid farewell to the prodigious priest and his gregarious friend. When I graduated to long pants, I started going to the races on Saturdays and these characters became forever entrenched in my mind as marvelous memories. Could I ever forget the day that Pete nearly picked the card?

On reflection I wasn't there, at all. It was one of those stories that morphs into legend. Pete used to be a system punter and this was a simple system. You just unloaded twenty bucks on a horse and doubled up for the rest of the program. You guessed it. He harpooned the first six winners and was eighty grand in front with one race to go. Over the years, Peter has had a peptic ulcer, a hip replacement, gout, psoriasis and the pox. But what about his heart? Picking the card is something that you hear about, but knowing someone who has actually done it! That's something else, again. This was against the law of averages, probability and decency.

In the end, he remained decent. His selection was beaten in a photo and he returned home to tell his wife that he had dropped twenty dollars at the track. A bad loss, as it turned out. He was apprehended, attempting to use his credit card on a tramcar.

– XII –

OTHER PEOPLE'S JOBS!

The Advisor!

The Reporters!

At this stage of my publication, many of you will be disappointed that I didn't study harder and become a brain surgeon or a rocket scientist, as my parents had hoped. These are the people with a clear head, who have their feet firmly on the ground and intend them to stay there.

The rest of you will appreciate my capacity to assimilate in a new country and parlay a noble vocation into a mish-mash of part-time jobs and scurrilous pursuits. I am sure that my ultimate career path was born from dissatisfaction and propagated by envy. Let us be honest, here. We all yearn for somebody else's job, but if you are not up to it, the only way is down.

THE ADVISOR!

When you only know one thing, it is always difficult to change careers mid-stream. Those of you who have been retrenched, downsized or terminated will know what I am talking about. Heck, you may even have been in the television industry and been boned. Now, that is painful. But, Dermot wasn't even thirty years of age. That is very young to be an unfrocked priest.

I know that you are not interested in any of the sordid details concerning his fall from grace so I won't be tiresome. Let's pick up the story on a dreary, smog-filled afternoon on Sunset Boulevard. The Depression was over and California was the place to be. The movie industry was in full swing and captivating everyone. Dermot was meeting with Light Fingers Larry Ladowski, who we both had known for years. Larry the Lad used to take up the Sunday collection at St Monica's, a rustic little church in the San Fernando Valley. He also collected union dues over at MGM and knew practically everybody, including Louis B. Mayer. So, the introduction was made.

Evidently, the studio was having problems with a young rising star on loan from Warner Bros. The movie mogul was looking for someone with impeccable credentials and Dermot was put on the payroll. Who would have guessed it? Spiritual Advisor to Errol Flynn!

Errol originated from Tasmania and he claimed Fletcher Christian as a distant relative. That's about as close as he came to being a Christian. By coincidence, he was chosen to portray Fletcher in the 1933 film *In the Wake of the Bounty*. I have read that he was also related to the real Robin Hood but I think he accepted this role because he liked to dress in tights. It all happened in quick succession – *Robin Hood*, *Don Juan*, *General Custer* and *Captain Blood*. He was the swashbuckler with a cutting cutlass and a rapier wit. The ladies seem to think that he also had an eminently photogenic rear end. Errol liked his whisky old and his women young and his best off-screen line was unforgettable. "It isn't what they say about you. It's what they whisper."

You can see that the padre's work was cut out. Not that he was paid any disrespect. In fact, the studio hardly paid him at all. We had to get Light Fingers Larry to tickle the kitty occasionally. On Dermot's watch, Errol managed to become the defendant in three statutory rape trials and was also married three times. His second wife used to work the snack counter at the courthouse and met him during one of his trials. Begorrah and be gosh! The man couldn't help himself. I would have liked to assist but I was busy enough elsewhere. Florenz Ziegfield was doing a stage version of *The Belles of St. Mary's* and I was giving tap dancing lessons for the nuns who were in the chorus. Little did I know that our leading lady was sneaking off for numerous trysts with Flynn. I should have guessed it. That song "Let's Tryst Again" was completely out of context with the rest of the show.

This was one movie star who couldn't reconcile his gross habits with his net income. In 1945, he was pulling two hundred thousand dollars a picture. His outlays for booze, broads, opium and court appearances often outstripped that. He was the quintessential Tasmanian Devil. Most people thought that he was Irish so naturally, he was a hell-raiser. Although Errol was frequently lectured on sex before marriage, alcohol and drug abuse, he moved from one excess to another. When he discovered sailing, we all thought that this might transform him. Unfortunately, he was discovered with two underage nymphets and Louis Mayer wanted to know whether his spiritual advisor was expecting a bonus that year. Mercifully, they didn't find Dermot down aft with the other two nymphets.

It's always difficult to admit that you are a failure. The priest moved on to peripheral work with Bella Lugosi and eventually was shown the door. To this day, he doesn't regret the time he spent trying to curb Errol's wicked, wicked ways. Regrettably, the movie star's influence has been quite profound. Dermot has now been married six times himself but alas, he no longer looks good in tights.

THE REPORTERS!

My fellow writers and journalist friends often ask me where I get the fire in my belly to keep coming up with the kind of perceptive, erudite commentary that continues to amaze and stupefy my most ardent fans. I suppose I have to go back to the time when I was toting tamales for my dear old dad in Memphis. I was happy enough but Pa wanted something better for me. He managed to call in a few favors and I soon found myself in the big city, working as a cub reporter for the Daily Planet, one of the most famous newspaper organizations in the world.

The Editor was a grumpy old coot. His name was Perry White. There was also a dame, Lois Lane, who was a bit of a looker and a nerdy sort of bloke called Clark Kent. Sadly, Lois treated me like the fresh-faced kid that I was. I didn't even drink beer. My God! What kind of reporter was I?

Kent and Lane both had a nose for a good story but the former was the one who always got the best scoops. It later transpired that he had some sort of X-ray vision and his typing speed was two thousand times the average. Nevertheless, I always thought that he was a man forever on the edge. Once, he was discovered in a telephone booth in his underpants. At this time, telephone sex was in its infancy but there were quite a few operators who did a very acceptable Mae West impression.

The Daily Planet was not listed as being owned by William Randolph Hearst, but it was. If Citizen Hearst didn't like you, you were probably a communist and he was very big on morality. He was very proud of his chain of newspapers and didn't take to criticism very well. The undoubted star of our newspaper was the comic-strip heroine *Little Orphan Annie*. I'll never forget the day that all hell broke loose. The doyen of the radio waves, a chap called Stan Freberg, intimated that Annie had a hygiene problem and that she was not a good example for the children of America. Evidently, she had worn the same little red dress over 7,564 consecutive editions. I believe Mr Hearst really saw red that day.

His stance on morality probably tempered the relationship between our best two reporters. Blind Freddy could tell that there was some kind of sexual tension going on there and although some of the girls put it about that Kent was a man of steel, I thought that he was a bit of a wimp. Incidentally, none of those girls put it about in my direction. I was a very frustrated correspondent.

Clark was definitely a bit of a loner and for some reason he always took his holidays at the North Pole and he wasn't a skier. I remember the day he returned for the Single Man's Race at the staff picnic and surprised everyone by blousing Smith and Wesson, in record time. These were our young guns, who went on to become very competent crime reporters. He was so fast they had to eat his dust. Just as they went on to be competent scribes, so did I. Of course, it's all down to confidence. You start off trying to jump puddles and in no time at all, you feel you can leap tall buildings. I think it was Clark who gave me that philosophical gem.

My greatest disappointment is that I have never won a journalistic award. That's because, when push comes to shove, there is always somebody there to upstage you. During the time of Watergate, I went to see *Deep Throat* five times but she didn't say a thing. I was that close to a Pulitzer Prize. The ensuing years have not been kind. Neither have my editors. They sent me to flower shows, sheep dog trials, eisteddfods and local county fairs. They made me a war correspondent at a time when there were no wars.

I still feel that I have one more story in me and perhaps it is your story. If you are a hero, a drug-riddled sports person or a politician with a dubious past, I can guarantee you front page coverage. But please do your worst before next Friday. If nothing better comes along, I have a tentative commitment to attend the Annual General Meeting of the South West Orchid Appreciation Society. I am sure that I will cover it brilliantly!

– XIII –

THE LAST WORD!

Justification!

There are some people who live for the moment and others who are entrenched in the past. There is no prize for guessing where I sit. I am told that there is good professional help for sad cases like mine and this is indeed encouraging. In the old days, they didn't know what to do with folks like us. If you didn't fit the mould, you ended up in advertising or journalism.

As I prepare to ride off into the sunset, I am satisfied that you know more about me than you did before. You will still have many questions. Some of you will want to know where to go to get a refund and I would love to tell you where to go. For the others, I would be very honored if you choose to retain this modest compilation as part of your own library. Just slip it in somewhere between your *Hannibal Lecter* collection and *Gone with the Wind*.

JUSTIFICATION!

Words! It is hard to know why we say the things that we do. When you write them down, it is even harder to disown them. I represent a singular group of like-minded individuals who universally maintain our unalienable right to color our commentary with rudimentary embellishment, fantasy and whimsical imagination. Often, this type of hyperbole is absorbed with cynicism and disbelief by the reader. By way of explanation, I refer to the assorted works of that Caribbean exile Ian Fleming.

Fleming saw his infamous hero, MI6 agent James Bond as a pretentious, patronizing Brit. Picky and pedantic! A twenty-four karat snob, by all accounts! Come on! Does anybody really take their Vodka Martini shaken not stirred? It makes no bloody difference. OK! I like my eggs sunny-side up but that's because I always look on the bright side of life.

It is not uncommon for writers to incorporate their own habitual idiosyncrasies into the persona of their major characters. Colombo, that irritating little detective, always wore a crumpled raincoat. Oscar Madison, from the *Odd Couple*, was also untidy and Inspector Rex had this insatiable appetite for ham rolls. However, I suspect that the latter predilection was a last-minute television addition as I believe that Rex was Jewish.

In recent times, a number of best selling authors have been exposed for fabricating their life experience and the literary community has not been impressed. This is something that I do on a daily basis but no-one seems remotely interested. I suppose that this is the small poppy syndrome in action. When I am in action I always feel morally bound to provide my readers with informative comment and endeavor to stimulate their sense of humor and engage their everyday passions. These are the things that get me going and I am modest enough to think that I truly represent the antithesis of the average Joe. This has been confirmed by my contemporaries who have often categorized me as a very average person.

If I am a man of the people, I wear this mantle of responsibility with pride and humility. After all, I am just like you. I scratch my butt, fiddle my income tax and doodle desperate maidens, whenever possible. It is true that my life journey is a lot more exciting than yours and that is why I couldn't live with myself if I didn't try to perk up your otherwise boring day.

Actually, I do live with myself and that is because co-habitation has proved to be less than appealing to those who may have had the opportunity. Nevertheless, I am an expert on personal relationships, animals, travel, fine dining and sport in general. Some would say that it is obscene that I am paid cash money for the kind of advice that I dole out but please don't be upset. With the exchange rate as it is, it is hardly anything.

Why am I trying to justify my existence? Perhaps it is that inferiority complex coming back after all these years. I can remember when I wouldn't say boo to a bobcat. I am sure that my shrink would say that I have been overtaken by repressed memories of bad experiences. Yes, I did experience a difficult childhood. When I was five years of age, I was kidnapped during my holidays in the Casbah. For a while, it looked like the ransom wasn't going to be paid, but in the end, my mom won the day. In the meantime, I attended a special school for transitory infidels in Cairo. Believe me, this was a tough gig for a blue eyed boy from Down Under. Today, that school is probably run by Al Qaeda.

My parents should never have let me vacation alone but it was a different world in those days. If James Bond had been around, I'm sure that he would have rescued me. Nevertheless, I remained resolute then as I am today. Shaken but not stirred!

Printed in the United States
By Bookmasters